King Ink II

Nick Cave

King Ink II first published by:

BLACK SPRING PRESS, Ltd.
63 Harlescott Rd.
London SE15 3DA
UNITED KINGDOM

All lyrics written by Nick Cave except:
"Henry Lee" Traditional/Cave
"Tread Softy (In Love)" Lane/Cave

Nick Cave and The Bad Seeds recordings
are available on Mute Records

Contents

TENDER PREY

The Mercy Seat
Up Jumped The Devil
Deanna
Watching Alice
Mercy
City of Refuge
Slowly Goes the Night
Sunday's Slave
Sugar Sugar Sugar
New Morning

The Mercy Seat

It began when they come took me from my home
And put me in Dead Row
Of which I am nearly wholly innocent you know
And I'll say it again
I...am...not...afraid...to...die

I began to warm and chill
To objects and their fields
A ragged cup, a twisted mop
The face of Jesus in my soup
Those sinister dinner meals
The meal trolley's wicked wheels
A hooked bone rising from my food
All things either good or ungood

And the mercy seat is waiting
And I think my head is burning
And in a way I'm yearning
To be done with all this measuring of truth
An eye for an eye
A tooth for a tooth
And anyway I told the truth
And I'm not afraid to die

Interpret signs and catalogue
A blackened tooth, a scarlet fog
The walls are bad. Black. Bottom kind
They are the sick breath at my hind
They are the sick breath at my hind
They are the sick breath at my hind
They are the sick breath gathering at my hind

I hear stories from the chamber
How Christ was born into a manger
And like some ragged stranger
Died upon the cross

And might I say it seems so fitting in its way
He was a carpenter by trade
Or at least that's what I'm told

My good hand tattooed E.V.I.L.
Across its brother's fist
That filthy five! They did nothing to challenge or resist

In Heaven His throne is made of gold
The ark of His testament is stowed
A throne from which I'm told
All history does unfold
Down here it's made of wood and wire
And my body is on fire
And God is never far away

Into the mercy seat I climb
My head is shaved, my head is wired
And like a moth that tries
To enter the bright eye
I go shuffling out of life
Just to hide in death awhile
And anyway I never lied

My kill-hand is called E.V.I.L.
Wears a wedding band that's G.O.O.D.
'Tis a long-suffering shackle
Collaring all that rebel blood

And the mercy seat is waiting
And I think my head is burning
And in a way I'm yearning
To be done with all this measuring of truth
An eye for an eye
And a tooth for a tooth
And anyway I told the truth
And I'm not afraid to die

And the mercy seat is burning
And I think my head is glowing
And in a way I'm hoping
To be done with all this weighing up of truth
An eye for an eye
And a tooth for a tooth
And I've got nothing left to lose
And I'm not afraid to die

And the mercy seat is glowing
And I think my head is smoking
And in a way I'm hoping
To be done with all these looks of disbelief
An eye for an eye
And a tooth for a tooth
And anyway there was no proof
Nor a motive why

And the mercy seat is smoking
And I think my head is melting
And in a way I'm hoping
To be done with all this twisting of the truth
A lie for a lie
And a truth for a truth
And I've got nothing left to lose
And I'm not afraid to die

And the mercy seat is melting
And I think my blood is boiling
And in a way I'm spoiling
All the fun with all this truth and consequence
An eye for an eye
And a truth for a truth
And anyway I told the truth
And I'm not afraid to die

And the mercy seat is waiting
And I think my head is burning
And in a way I'm yearning
To be done with all this measuring of proof
A life for a life
And a truth for a truth
And anyway there was no proof
But I'm not afraid to tell a lie

And the mercy seat is waiting
And I think my head is burning
And in a way I'm yearning
To be done with all this measuring of truth
An eye for an eye
And a truth for a truth
And anyway I told the truth
But I'm afraid I told a lie

Say had bound been ~~tyed~~ with electrical tape. He'd used a gag.
so times. ~~Her killer had used a~~

killing ~~death~~, same as my wifes

JOHN MILTON 1608-1674

THE RISING WATERS DARK + DEEP.

AND THAT 2-handed engine at the door stands ready to smite once + smite no more.

ABOVE THE SMOKE + STIR of this dim spot, ~~that~~ which men call earth.

THE UNSUNNED HEAPS OF MISERS TREASURE

UNDER the RIBS OF DEATH

FRAGILE

AC-343

in?

7

Up Jumped The Devil

O my, O my
What a wretched life
I was born on the day
That my poor mother died
I was cut form her belly
With a Stanley knife
My Daddy did a jig
With the drunk midwife

Who's that yonder all in flames
Dragging behind him a sack of chains
Who's that yonder all in flames
Up jumped the Devil and he staked his claim

O poor heart
I was doomed from the start
Doomed to play
The villain's part
I was the baddest Johnny
In the apple cart
My blood was blacker
Than the chambers of a dead nun's heart

Who's that milling on the courthouse steps
Nailing my face to the hitching fence
Who's that milling on the courthouse steps
Up jumped the Devil and off he crept

O no, O no
Where could I go
With my hump of trouble
And my sack of woe
To the digs and deserts of Mexico
Where my neck was safe from the lynching rope

Who's that yonder laughing at me
Like I was the brunt of some hilarity
Who's that yonder laughing at me
Up jumped the Devil 1,2,3

Ha ha ha
How lucky we were
We hit the cathouse
And sampled their wares
We got as drunk
As a couple of Czars
One night I spat out
My lucky stars

Who's that dancing on the jailhouse roof
Stamping on the ramping with a cloven hoof
Who's that dancing on the jailhouse roof
Up jumped the Devil and said, "Here is your man and I got proof"

O no, don't go, O no
O slow down, Joe
The righteous path
Is straight as an arrow
Take a walk
And you'll find it too narrow
Too narrow for the likes of me

Who's that hanging from the gallow tree
His eyes are hollow but he looks like me
Who's that hanging from the gallow tree
Up jumped the Devil and took my soul from me

Down we go, down we go
The Devil and me
Down we go, down we go
To Eternity
Down we go, down we go
We go down down down down down ad inferno

DEVILS
LEVELS
REVELS
SEVERS

B C D F G H J K L M N P Q R S T V W Z

FRI
SAT
SUN
MON
TUES
WED.

Deanna

O DEANNA
O Deanna!
O DEANNA
Sweet Deanna!
O DEANNA
You know you are my friend, yeah
O DEANNA
And I ain't down here for your money
I ain't down here for your love
I ain't' down here for your love or money
I'm down here for your soul

No carpet on the floor
And the winding-cloth holds many moths
Around your Ku Klux furniture
I cum a death's-head in your frock
We discuss the murder pact
We discuss the murder and the murder act
Murder takes the wheel of the Cadillac
And death climbs in the back

O DEANNA
This is a car
O DEANNA
This is a gun
O DEANNA
And this is day number one
O DEANNA
Our little crime-worn histories
Black and smoking Christmas trees
And honey, it ain't a mystery
Why you're a mystery to me

We will eat out of their pantries
And their parlours
Ashy leavings in their beds
And we'll unload until their heads
In this mean season
This little angel that I squeezin'
She ain't been mean to me

O DEANNA
O Deanna!
O DEANNA
You are my friend and my partner
O DEANNA
On this house on the hill
O DEANNA
And I ain't' down here for your money
I ain't down here for your love
I ain't down here for your love or money
I'm down here for your soul

O DEANNA
I am a-knocking
O DEANNA
With my toolbox and my stocking
O DEANNA
And I'll meet you on the corner
O DEANNA
Yes, you point it like a finger
O DEANNA
And squeeze its little thing
O DEANNA
Feel its kick, hear its bang
And let's not worry about its issue
Don't worry about where it's been
And don't worry about where it hits
'Cause it just ain't yours to sin

O DEANNA
No, it just ain't yours to sin
O DEANNA
Sweet Deanna
O DEANNA
And we ain't getting any younger
O DEANNA
And I don't intend gettin' any older
O DEANNA
The sun a hump at my shoulder

O DEANNA
O Deanna!
O DEANNA
Sweet Deanna
O DEANNA
And I ain't down here for your money
I ain't down here for your love
I ain't down here for your love or money
I'm down here for your soul

Watching Alice

Alice wakes
It is morning
She is yawning
As she walks about the room
Her hair falls down her breast
She is naked and it is June
Standing at the window
I wonder if she knows that I can see
Watching Alice rise year after year
Up in her palace, she's captive there

Alice's body
Is golden brown
Her hair hangs down
As she brushes it one hundred times
First she pulls her stockings on
And then the church bell chimes
Alice climbs into her uniform
The zipper's on the side
Watching Alice dressing in her room
It's so depressing, it's cruel

Watching Alice dressing in her room
It's so depressing, it's true

Mercy

I stood in the water
In the middle month of winter
My camel skin was torture
I was in a state of nature
The wind, sir, it was wicked
I was so alone
Just as I predicted
My followers were gone

And I cried, "Mercy
Have mercy on me"
And I got down on my knees

Thrown into a dungeon
Bread and water was my portion
Faith—my only weapon
To rest the Devil's legion
The speak-hole would slide open
A viper's voice would plead
Thick with innuendo
Syphillis and greed

And she cried, "Mercy
Have mercy on me"
And I told her to get down on her knees

In a garden full of roses
My hands were tied behind me
My cousin was working miracles
I wondered if he'd find me
The moon was turned toward me
Like a platter made of gold
My death, it almost bored me
So often was it told

And I cried, "Mercy"
I cried, "Mercy on me"
Crying, "Mercy
Have mercy on me"

City Of Refuge

You better run
You better run and run and run
You better run, you better run
You better run to the City of Refuge
You better run, you better run
You better run to the City of Refuge

You stand before your maker
In a state of shame
Because your robes are covered in mud
While you kneel at the feet
Of a woman of the street
The gutters will run with blood
They will run with blood!

You better run, you better run
You better run to the City of Refuge
You better run, you better run
You better run to the City of Refuge

In the days of madness
My brother, my sister
When you're dragged toward the Hell-mouth
You will beg for the end
But there ain't gonna be one, friend
For the grave will spew you out
It will spew you out!

You better run, you better run
You better run to the City of Refuge
You better run, you better run
You better run to the City of Refuge

You'll be working in the darkness
Against your fellow man
And you'll find you're called to come forth
So you'll scrub and you'll scrub
But the trouble is, bud
The blood won't wash off
No, it won't come off!

You better run, you better run
You better run to the City of Refuge

You better run, you better run
You better run and run and run
You better run to the City of Refuge

THE
IN LIGHT OF TRUTH
THE GRAIL MESSAGE
Rogue Valley
ABD-RU-SHIN

Slowly Goes The Night

Lover, lover, goodbye
So slowly goes the night
I trace the print of your body with my hand
Like the map of some forbidden land
I trace the ghosts of your bones
With my trembling hand
Dark is my night
But darker is my day, yeah
I must've been blind
Out of my mind
Not to read the warning signs
How goes it?
It goes lonely
Goes slowly

So slowly goes the night
Ten lonely days, ten lonely nights
I watch the moon get flayed anew
Until the moon becomes the skinning tool
I send the skins of my sins out to cover and comfort you
I know of a Heaven
And honey I know of a Hell, yeah
I hang my head
In my bed
And remember what you said
"One evening, I'm leaving"
And I laughed and checked her breathing

Go slowly through the night
O baby, I feel the heal of time
I wake to find you sitting there
Cutting tangles out of your hair
Singing a song that's all wrong
Hey, but that's alright, I don't care

O darling, forgive me
For all the misery, yeah
I embrace an empty space
And your laughing song it fades

Where goes it?
It goes some place
Where it's lonely

And black as the night
Come back, darling and put things right
I hang my head and cry cry cry
Darling, all night I try
To seize on a reason for this mad mad season
The nights, they are so long now
I can't remember it being light
Call it sleep, call it death, call it what you like
But only sleep, dear
Only sleep brings you back to life, yeah
I hang my head
I toss and I sweat
I never never can forget
How goes it?
I'm going, but slowly slowly going
And we both know that it's gonna be alright

But it ain't you who has to cry cry cry
Ten lonely days, ten lonely nights
Since you left my side side side

Sunday's Slave

Sunday's got a slave
Monday's got one too
Sunday's got a slave
Monday's got one too
Our sufferings are countless
Our pleasures are a motley few
Spend all day digging my grave
Now go get Sunday's slave

Tuesday sleeps in the stable
Wednesday's in chains
Tuesday gathers up the crumbs under the table
Wednesday dare not complain
My heart has collapsed on the tracks of a run-away train
Just whisper his name
And here comes Sunday's slave

The hands in the stable are willing and able to pay
If you feel at a loss, man, as to who is the boss-man
Ask the blood on one of its bad days
For his nerve is to serve but the service is a mockery
He insists that he piss in your fist
But he still takes the money anyway
The master's a bastard
But don't tell Sunday's slave

Thursday's angered the master
OK, so Friday's gonna pay
Thursday's angered the master
Yeah, so Friday's gonna pay
One night on the rack and he's back saddling up Saturday
You can only whisper his name
But no on Sundays
Never on Sundays
O not on Sunday's slave

Sugar Sugar Sugar

Sugar sugar sugar
That man is bad
The road he drives you down
O sugar, it's a drag

That road it twists
That road is crossed
It's down that road
A lot of little girls go lost

Sugar sugar sugar
Keep on driving on
Until the City of Right
Becomes the City of Wrong

That stretch is long
You'll slip and slide
That stretch will find you
Gagged and tied

The hunger lies
In a lowly ditch
His eyes they sting
And his fingers twitch

You'll be his queen for the night
But in the morning you'll wake
With the lords and high ladies
Of the bottom of the lake

Sugar sugar sugar
That man is wild
And sugar, you know
That you're merely a child

He will laugh
And hang your sheets to see
The tokens of your virginity

Sugar sugar sugar
Honey, you're so sweet
And beside you, baby
Nothing can compete

Sugar sugar sugar
Honey, you're so sweet
But beside you, baby
A bad man sleeps

You better pray baby
Pray baby, pray baby
You better pray
You better pray baby
Pray baby, pray baby
You better pray baby

Sugar sugar sugar
That man is bad
And that's the bottom, baby
Coming right up ahead

You can smell his fear
You can smell his love
As he wipes his mouth
On your altar cloth

Sugar sugar sugar
Try to understand
I'm an angel of God
I'm your guardian

He smells your innocence
And like a dog he comes
And like all the dogs he is
I shut him down

Sugar sugar sugar
I can't explain
Must I kill that cocksucker
Every day

You better pray baby, pray baby, pray baby
You better pray your daddy he ain't far away
You better pray baby, pray baby, pray baby
You better pray your daddy's come to take you away
You better pray baby, pray baby, pray baby
You better pray O tender prey baby, tender prey
You better pray tender prey baby, tender prey

New Morning

One morn I awakened
A new sun was shining
The sky was a Kingdom
All covered in blood
The moon and the stars
Were the troops that lay conquered
Like fruit left to wither
Poor spiritual food

And the spears of the bright sun
All brave with its conquest
Did hover unearthly
In banners of fire
I knelt in the garden
Awash with the dawning
And a voice came so brightly
I covered my eyes

Thank you for giving
This bright new morning
So steeped seemed the evening
In darkness and blood
There'll be no sadness
There'll be no sorrow
There'll be no road too narrow
There'll be a new day
And it's today
For us

SHE ~~HAD~~ WRISTS WHICH, DID HER BANGLES
NOT CONTAIN
WOULD RUN OUT HER SLEEVES ~~LIKE~~ IN SILVERN
RAIN

GOODNIGHT + SLEEP TIGHT + SWEET
DREAMS

Girl At The Bottom Of My Glass

Well, I can't raise my glass
Without seeing her ass
Through its telescopic bottom
I can't raise my glass
Without seeing her ass
Through its telescopic bottom
If you wanna know what animal it is
Ask the girl at the bottom of my glass

Well, lover come a-knocking
With my toolbag and my stocking
[...]
Well, lover come a-knocking
With my toolbag and my stocking
[...]
If you wanna know what's shaking down the house
Ask the girl at the bottom of my glass

I can't spill my drink
Without the woman at the sink
Coming round in her rubber mittens
I can't slop my drink
Without that woman at the sink
Coming at me in her rubber mittens
If you're looking for the woman of the house
Ask the girl at the bottom of my glass

I can't raise my drink
Without stopping to think
That some bad baby's giving me trouble
I can't rise my drink
Without stopping to think
That some bad baby's giving me trouble
If you wanna see what's inside of Sally
You'll find that girl in a hole out in the alley

I can't raise my glass
Without seeing her ass
This booze is turning bitter
I can't raise my glass
Without seeing her ass
I'm gonna jump right up and hit her

Well, you wanna know a little about my past
Take a squitch at the bitch in my house

THE GOOD SON

Foi Na Cruz
The Good Son
Sorrow's Child
The Weeping Song
The Ship Song
The Hammer Song
Lament
The Witness Song
Lucy

(I'll Love You) Till The End Of The World

Foi Na Cruz

Foi na cruz, foi na cruz
Que um dia
Meus pecados castigados em Jesus
Foi na cruz
Que um dia
Foi na cruz

Love comes a-knocking
Comes a-knocking upon our door
But you, you and me, love
We don't live there any more

Foi na cruz, foi na cruz
Que um dia
Meus pecados castigados em Jesus
Foi na cruz
Que um dia
Foi na cruz

A little sleep, a little slumber
A little folding of the hands to sleep
A little love, a little hate, babe
A little trickery and deceit

Foi na cruz, foi na cruz
Que um dia
Meus pecados castigados em Jesus
Foi na cruz
Que um dia
Foi na cruz

Dream on 'til you can dream no more
For all our grand plans, babe
Will be dreams forever more

Foi na cruz, foi na cruz
Que um dia
Meus pecados castigados em Jesus
Foi na cruz
Que um dia
Foi na cruz

Foi na cruz, foi na cruz
Que um dia
Meus pecados castigados em Jesus
Foi na cruz
Que um dia
Foi na cruz

The Good Son

One more man gone
One more man gone
One more man is gone
The good son walks into the field
He is a tiller, he has a tiller's hands
But down in his heart now
He lays down queer plans
Against his brother and against his family
Yet he worships his brothers
And he worships his mother
But it's his father, he says, is an unfair man
The good son
The good son
The good son

The good son has sat and often wept
Beneath a malign star by which he's kept
And the night-time in which he's wrapped
Speaks of good and speaks of evil
And he calls to his mother
And he calls to his father
But they are deaf in the shadows of his brother's truancy
The good son
The good son
The good son

And he curses his mother
And he curses his father
And he curses his virtue like an unclean thing
The good son
The good son
The good son

One more man gone
One more man gone
One more man
One more man gone
One more man gone
One more man
One more man gone
One more man gone
One more man

One more man gone
One more man gone
One more man
One more man gone
One more man gone
One more man
One more man gone
One more man gone
One more man

Sorrow's Child

Sorrow's child
Sits by the river
Sorrow's child
Hears not the water
Sorrow's child
Sits by the river
Sorrow's child
Hears not the water
And just when it seems as though
You've got strength enough to stand
Sorrow's child all weak and strange
Stands waiting at your hand
Sorrow's child
Steps in the water
Sorrow's child
You follow after
Sorrow's child
Wades in deeper
Sorrow's child
Invites you under
And just when you thought as though
All your tears were wept and done
Sorrow's child grieves not what has passed
But all the past still yet to come
Sorrow's child
Sits by the water
Sorrow's child
Your arms enfold her
Sorrow's child
You're loathe to befriend her
Sorrow's child
But in sorrow surrender
And just when it seems as though
All your tears were at an end
Sorrow's child lifts up her hand
And she brings it down again

Your wayward eyes
go wandering by
And my world grows thundery dark
~~but there go your eyes a-roaming~~

~~I'll wait for the day~~
I'll be patient + gay
As I wait for the day
That they finally find their mark

jenny
LISA —
prayers
(junkmail)

rain ringing on the rooftops
as she storms away

~~BIG~~ ~~SINKING~~

PINK SUN IN AN IVORY SKY
MY GIRL'S DRESS IN THE WIND DOES FLY
PINK SUN SINKS IN AN IVORY SKY
MY GIRLS DRESS IN THE WIND DOES FLY
RAIN RINGING ON THE ROOFTOPS
AS SHE STORMS GOODBYE (away)
(my girl) (waves) (says)

(remember)

good
There's a hole in my side
a hiss in my ear
and a I got a awful belly ache

ultimate
untimely

hissing
belly-ache
[illegible]

Can't stop the sun from setting
Can't prevent the night's fall

a snake, a
See
rib + an apple

The fruits in the garden are
But they can give you a belly-ache

I
I was having + eating a cake
A rib, an apple and a snake

I'm a man
She's female to the core
(a woman)

NEXT PAGE

The Weeping Song

Go, son, go down to the water
And see the women weeping there
Then go up into the mountains
The men, they are weeping too

Father, why are all the women weeping?
They are weeping for their men
Then why are all the men there weeping?
They are weeping back at them

This is a weeping song
A song in which to weep
While all the men and women sleep
This is a weeping song
But I won't be weeping long

Father, why are all the children weeping?
They are merely crying, son
O are they merely crying, father?
Yes, true weeping is yet to come

This is a weeping song
A song in which to weep
While all the little children sleep
This is a weeping song
But I won't be weeping long

O father, tell me, are you weeping?
Your face seems wet to touch
O then I'm so sorry, father
I never thought I hurt you so much

This is a weeping song
A song in which to weep
While we rock ourselves to sleep
This is a weeping song
But I won't be weeping long
No, I won't be weeping long
No, I won't be weeping long
No, I won't be weeping long
No, I won't be weeping long

The Ship Song

Come sail your ships around me
And burn your bridges down
We make a little history, baby
Every time you come around

Come loose your dogs upon me
And let your hair hang down
You are a little mystery to me
Everytime you come around

We talk about it all night long
We define our moral ground
But when I crawl into your arms
Everything comes tumbling down

Come sail your ships around me
And burn your bridges down
We make a little history, baby
Every time you come around

Your face has fallen sad now
For you know the time is nigh
When I must remove your wings
And you, you must try to fly

Come sail your ships around me
And burn your bridges down
We make a little history, baby
Every time you come around

Come loose your dogs upon me
And let your hair hang down
You are a little mystery to me
Everytime you come around

The Hammer Song

I set out on Monday
The night was cold and vast
And my brother slept
And though I left quite quietly
My father raged and raged
And my mother wept

Now my life was like a river
All sucked into the ground
And then the hammer came down
Lord, the hammer came down

Many miles did I roam
Through the ice and through the snow
My horse died on the seventh day

I stumbled into a city
Where the people tried to kill me
And I ran in shame
Then I came upon a river
And I laid my saddle down
And then the hammer came down
Lord, the hammer came down
It knocked me to the ground
And I said, "Please, please
Take me back to my hometown"
Lord, the hammer came down

Now I've been made weak by visions
Many visions did I see
All through the night

On the seventh hour an angel came
With many snakes in all his hands
And I fled in fright

I pushed off into the river
And the water came around
And then the hammer came down
Lord, the hammer came down
And it did not make a sound
And I said, "Please, please
Take me back to my home ground"
Lord, the hammer came down

YOU CAN'T NAIL A GOOD MAN DOWN

You can't nail a good man down
No matter how you try
All your Evil comes marching home
When you die

You can't nail a good man down
He'll soon get up + ~~go~~ leave
You wish you never ever tried
As you grieve

You can't nail a good man down
Even the Bible tells you so
You stand there with your hammers
Watching him go

You can't nail a good man down

letters - the fossils of feeling
they show me that you cared

Lament

I've seen your fairground hair
Your seaside eyes
Your vampire tooth, your little truth
Your tiny lies

I know your trembling hand, your guilty prize
Your sleeping limbs, your foreign hymns
Your midnight cries

So dry your eyes
And turn your head away
Now there's nothing more to say
Now you're gone away

I know your trail of tears, your slip of hand
Your monkey paw, your monkey claw
And your monkey hand

I've seen your trick of blood, your trap of fire
Your ancient wound, your scarlet moon
And your jailhouse smile

So dry your eyes
And turn your head away
Now there's nothing more to say
Now you're gone away

I'll miss your urchin smile, your orphan tears
Your shining prize, your tiny cries
Your little fears

I'll miss your fairground hair,
Your seaside eyes
Your vampire tooth, your little truth
And your tiny lies

So dry your eyes
And turn your head away
Now there's nothing more to say
Now you're gone away

So dry your eyes
And turn your head away
Now there's nothing more to say
Now you're gone away

The Witness Song

Yeah, yeah
Well, well
I took a walk down to the port
Where strangers meet and do consort
All blinkered with desire
And a winter fog moved thickly on
A winter fog moved thickly on
A winter fog moved thickly on

Now who will be the witness
When the fog's too thick to see

And I saw a friend beside a wall
Her hands were raised in suplication
And her face I could not see at all
And I raised my hands in rage
And brought them down again
And we entered through the eastern door
And I entered through the eastern door
And she entered through the eastern door

Now who will be the witness
When you're all too blind to see
O yes, yes, yes

And time gets somewhat muddied here
But no matter, no matter
Here come the events all tumbling down
Now beyond the wall was a great garden
Into which we passed
Me and my friend
And the place was all overgrown with weeds
And behold from its centre there rose a great fountain
The fountain with the healing waters
And we knelt down by the rim

And I dipped my hand in
And she dipped her hand in too
And I said, "Are you healed?"
And she said, "Well, are you healed?"
And I said, "Yes, I'm healed"
And she said, "Well, yes, I'm healed then too"
And I said, "Babe, you are a liar"
"Babe, you are a liar"
"Babe, you are a liar, too"
Now, who will be the witness
When you're all too healed to see

And I kissed her once, I kissed her twice
And made my way to leave her
And she raised her hand up to her face
And brought it down again
I said, "That gesture, it will haunt me
That gesture, it will haunt me"
And I left there by the eastern door
She left there by the western door

Now who will be the witness there
When you're blind and you can't see
Who will be the witness there
When you're all so clean and you cannot see
Who will be the witness there
When your friends are everywhere
Who will be the witness there
And your enemies have ceased to care

Lucy

Last night I lay trembling
The moon it was low
It was the end of love
Of misery and woe

Then suddenly above me
Her face buried in light
Came a vision of beauty
All covered in white

Now the bell-tower is ringing
And the night has stole past
O Lucy, can you hear me?
Wherever you rest

I'll love her forever
I'll love her for all time
I'll love her 'til the stars
Fall down from the sky

Now the bell-tower is ringing
And I shake on the floor
O Lucy, can you hear me?
When I call and call

Now the bell-tower is ringing
And the moon it is high
O Lucy, can you hear me?
When I cry and cry and cry

(I'll Love You) Till The End Of The World

It was a miracle I even got out of Longwood alive—this town full of men with big mouths and no guts. I mean, if you can just picture it, the whole third floor of the hotel gutted by the blast. And the street below showered in shards of broken glass. And all the drunks pouring out of the dance halls staring up at the smoke and the flames. And the blind pencil-seller waving his stick, shouting for his dog that lay dead on the side of the road. And me, if you can believe this, at the wheel of the car, closing my eyes and actually praying. Not to God above, but to you. Saying,

"Help me girl, help me girl
I'll love you till the end of the world
With your eyes black as coal and your long dark curls"

Some things we plan, we sit and we invent and we plot and cook up. Others are works of inspiration, of poetry. And it was this genius hand that pushed me up the hotel stairs to say my last goodbye to her hair white as snow and her pale blue eyes, saying, "I gotta go, I gotta go, the bomb and the breadbasket are ready to blow." In this town of men with big mouths and no guts, the pencil-seller's dog, spooked by the explosion, leaping under my wheels, as I careened out of Longwood on my way to you, waiting in your dress, in your dress of blue.

And I said, "Thank you girl, thank you girl
I'll love you till the end of the world
With your eyes black as coal and your long dark curls"

And with the horses prancing through the fields, with my knife in my jeans and the rain on the shield, I sang a song for the glory of the beauty of you, waiting for me in your dress of blue.

"Thank you girl, thank you girl
I'll love you till the end of the world
With your eyes black as coal and your long dark curls"

I said, "Thank you girl, thank you girl
I'll love you till the end of the world
With your eyes black as coal and your long dark curls"

My spirit
committed to
My soul lies prostrate
DESCARTES
2nd thing he "knew"
A clear & distinct impression of God
1st thing → "I think therefore I am"
down
I am dragged to my knees
That is the way, babe
it seems
It seems that is the way
for my spirit
for me to be redeemed
must bleed
body
another
The piper must be paid, my babe
There is no other way

HENRY'S DREAM

Papa Won't Leave You, Henry
I Had A Dream, Joe
Straight To You
Brother, My Cup Is Empty
Christina The Astonishing
When I First Came To Town
John Finn's Wife
Loom Of the Land
Jack The Ripper

Faraway, So Close!
Cassiel's Song
Blue Bird

Papa Won't Leave You, Henry

I went out walking the other day
The wind hung wet around my neck
My head it rung with screams and groans
From the night I spent amongst her bones
I passed beside the mission house
Where that mad old buzzard, the Reverend,
Shrieked and flapped about life after you're dead
Well, I thought about my friend, Michel
How they rolled him in linoleum
And shot him in the neck
A bloody halo like a think-bubble
Circling his head
And I bellowed at the firmament
Looks like the rains are here to stay
And the rain pissed down upon me
And washed me all away
Saying,
Papa won't leave you, Henry
Papa won't leave you, Boy
Papa won't leave you, Henry
Papa won't leave you, Boy
Well, the road is long
And the road is hard
And many fall by the side
But Papa won't leave you, Henry
So there ain't no need to cry

And I went on down the road
He went on down the road
And I went on down the road
He went on down the road

Well, the moon it looked exhausted
Like something you should pity
Spent and age-spotted
Above the sizzling wires of the city

Well, it reminded me of her face
Her bleached and hungry eyes
Her hair was like a curtain
Falling open with the laughter
And closing with the lies
But the ghost of her still lingers on
Though she's passed through me and is gone
The slum dogs, they are barking
And the rain children on the streets
And the tears that we will weep today
Will all be washed way
By the tears that we will weep again tomorrow
Papa won't leave you, Henry
Papa won't leave you, Boy
Papa won't leave you, Henry
Papa won't leave you, Boy
For the road is long
And the road is hard
And many fall by the side
But Papa won't leave you, Henry
So there ain't no need to cry

And I went on down the road
He went on down the road
And I went on down the road
He went on down the road

And I came upon a little house
A little house upon a hill
And I entered through — the curtain hissed —
In the house with its blood-red bowels
Where wet-lipped women with greasy fists
Crawled the ceilings and the walls
They filled me full of drink
And led me round the rooms
Naked and cold and grinning
Until everything went black

And I came down spinning
I awoke so drunk and full of rage
That I could hardly speak
A fag in a whale-bone corset
Draping his dick across my cheek
And it's into the shame
And it's into the guilt
And it's into the fucking fray
And the walls ran red around me
A warm arterial spray
Saying,
Papa won't leave you, Henry
Papa won't leave you, Boy
Papa won't leave you, Henry
Papa won't leave you, Boy
Well, the night is dark
And the night is deep
And its jaws are open wide
But Papa won't leave you, Henry
So there ain't no need to cry

And I went on down the road
He went on down the road
And I went on down the road
He went on down the road

It's the rainy season where I'm living
Death comes leaping out of every doorway
Wasting you for your money, for your clothes
And for your nothing
Entire towns being washed away
Favelas, exploding on inflammable spillways
Lynch-mobs, death squads, babies being born without brains
The mad heat and the relentless rains
And if you stick your arm in that hole
It comes out sheared off to the bone
And with her kisses bubbling on my lips

I swiped the rain and nearly missed
And I went on down the road
He went on down the road
Singing,
Papa won't leave you, Henry
Papa won't leave you, Boy
Papa won't leave you, Henry
Papa won't leave you, Boy
Well, the road is long
And the road is hard
And many fall by the side
But Papa won't leave you, Henry
So there ain't no need to cry

And I went on down the road
He went on down the road
And I went on down the road
He went on down the road
Bent beneath my heavy load
Under his heavy load
Yeah, I went on down the road
Yeah, he went on down the road

Woah, woah
Woah, woah
Woah, woah
Woah, woah
And I went on down that road

I Had A Dream, Joe

I had a dream
I had a dream
I had a dream, Joe

I had a dream, Joe
You were standing in the middle of an open road
I had a dream, Joe
Your hands were raised up to the sky
And your mouth was covered in foam
I had a dream, Joe
A shadowy Jesus flitted from tree to tree
I had a dream, Joe
And a society of whores stuck needles in an image of me
I had a dream, Joe
It was Autumn time and thickly fell the leaves
And in that dream, Joe
A pimp in a seersucker suit sucked a toothpick
And pointed his finger at me

I had a dream
I had a dream
I had a dream, Joe

I opened my eyes, Joe
The night had been a giant, dribbling and pacing the boards
I opened my eyes, Joe
All your letters and cards stacked up against the door
I opened my eyes, Joe
The morning light came slowly tumbling through the crack
In the window, Joe
And I thought of you and I felt like I was lugging
A body on my back

I had a dream
I had a dream
I had a dream, Joe

Where did you go, Joe?
On that endless, senseless, demented drift
Where did you go, Joe?
Into the woods, into the tress, where you move and shift
where did you go, Joe?
All dressed up in your ridiculous seersucker suit
Where did you go, Joe?
With that strew of wreckage
Forever at the heel of your boot

I had a dream
I had a dream
I had a dream, Joe
I had a dream
I had a dream
I had a dream, Joe

Straight To You

All the towers of ivory are crumbling
And the swallows have sharpened their beaks
This is the time of our great undoing
This is the time that I'll come running
Straight to you
For I am captured
Straight to you
For I am captured
One more time

The light in our window is fading
The candle gutters on the ledge
Well, now, sorrow, it comes a-stealing
And I'll cry, girl, but I'll come a-running
Straight to you
For I am captured
Straight to you
For I am captured
One more time

Gone are the days of rainbows
Gone are the nights of swinging from the stars
For the sea will swallow up the mountains
And the sky will throw thunder-bolts and sparks
Straight at you
But I'll come a-running
Straight to you
But I'll come a-running
One more time

Heaven has denied us its kingdom
The saints are drunk and howling at the moon
The chariots of angels are colliding
Well, I'll run, babe, but I'll come running
Straight to you
For I am captured
Straight to you
For I am captured
One more time

I MISS YOU MORE THAN WORDS CAN TELL

ALL IS WILL. AND SO WE MAKE OUR CHOICE
WE ARE WHAT WE EMBRACE AND WE ARE WHAT WE RESIST.
"WE ARE STRONG" I SAID "BUT THE WILL IS MADE WEAK"
WITH ONE HAND YOU BRUSHED THE TEAR FROM MY CHEEK
IT WAS AN ACTION SO VERY FAMILIAR
AS TOUCHED ME IN PLACES I HAD FORGOT DID EXIST
AND HAIR HID MY LOOK OF LONGING AND NEED
AS YOU BENT YOUR BODY ACROSS ME AND KISSED
AND WE LAY TILL THE SUN AROSE
LEAVING ITS RESIDUE OF REMORSE AS IT
ACROSS THE ROOM AS YOU DRESSED + I
THE STRANDS OF YOUR GOLDEN HAIR FROM MY SHIRT WH
THE HOTEL DOOR CLOSED + YOU WERE GONE
AND I SAT THE TELEPHONE
WRAPPED IN THE COAT YOU'D PACKED FOR THE COLD
STILL TRAPPED WITH IN THE FABRIC YOUR SMELL
MY WILL IS WEAK BUT MY LOVE IS STRONG
+ GO
AND YOU ARE SO FAR + IT HAS BEEN SO LONG
I LOVE YOU + I HOPE YOU ARE WELL
I MISS YOU BABY I MISS YOU BABY
I MISS YOU MORE THAN WORDS CAN TELL

★ CECIL TAYLOR – Spring of two blue jays.

CDEFGHGRPRS

I CRY INTO THE TELEPHONE, PLEASE COME + FIND ME

~~[illegible]~~

SEEK ME OUT + WHEN YOU DO. WALK QUIETLY UP BEHIND ME

LET YOUR FORCE, LET ~~YOUR~~ PRESENCE SLOWLY ~~[illegible]~~ INVADE ME, HIT ME

+ WHEN I FINALLY TURN TO YOU, DO NOT TOUCH ME, I FORBID THEE (DO NOT SPEAK)

I HAVE WAITED ~~NOW~~ SO LONG + IN MY WAY I'VE SAVED MYSELF FOR YOU

THE RESIDUE OF REMORSE HANGS ABOVE ME, AND I DONT KNOW WHAT TO DO

SO I MOVE MY FINGERS TO YOU FACE HALF-EXPECTING THEM TO SIMPLY PASS ON THROUGH

MY DARLING MY WILL IS WEAK but SO VERY STRONG IS MY LOVE FOR YOU

DON'T SPEAK! LOOK YOU ARE CRYING + MY GOD IT SEEMS THAT I AM CRYING TOO

ACRID TASTE ~~[illegible]~~ OWN SWEET SMELL

LONGING HAS IT'S ~~OWN FLAVOUR~~, LONELINESS IT'S

~~IT~~ I MISSED YOU (BABY) MORE THAN WORDS CAN EVER ~~S~~TELL

I HAVE NOTHING MORE TO GIVE, I HAVE LITTLE LEFT TO SELL

~~I~~ JUST ~~MISS~~ MISSED YOU BABY MORE THAN WORDS COULD EVER TELL

CREPT YES I MISSED YOU BABY MORE THAN WORDS CAN TELL

GATHERED

ICH YOU WORE ~~WHEN YOU SLEPT~~

BILL

BELL RILL FELL FILL GILL HELL HILL MELL ~~MELL~~ (NIL) PILL PELL-MELL

QUILL SILL STILL - VILLE WELL WILL

Brother, My Cup Is Empty

Brother, my cup is empty
And I haven't got a penny
For to buy no more whiskey
I have to go home

I am the captain of my pain
Tis the bit, the bridle
The trashing cane
The stirrup, the harness
The whipping mane
The pickled eye
The shrinking brain
O brother, buy me one more drink
I'll explain the nature of my pain
Yes, let me tell you once again
I am the captain of my pain

O brother, my cup is empty
And I haven't got a penny
For to buy no more whiskey
I have to go home

I cannot blame it all on her
To blame her all would be a lie
For many a night I lay awake
And wished that I could watch her die
To see her accusing finger spurt
To see flies swarm her hateful eye
To watch her groaning in the dirt
To see her clicking tongue crack dry
O brother, buy me one more drink
One more drink and then goodbye
And do not mock me when I say
Let's drink one more before I die

O brother, my cup is empty
And I haven't got a penny
For to buy no more whiskey
I have to go home

Well, I've been sliding down on rainbows
I've been swinging from the stars
Now this wretch in beggar's clothing
Bangs his cup across the bars
Look, this cup of mine is empty!
Seems I've misplaced my desires
Seems I'm sweeping up the ashes
Of all my former fires
So brother, be a brother
And fill this tiny cup of mine
And please, sir, make it whiskey
For I have no head for wine

O brother, my cup is empty
And I haven't got a penny
For to buy no more whiskey
I have to go home

I counted up my blessings
And I counted only one
One tiny little blessing
And now that blessing's gone
So buy me one more drink, my brother
Then I'm taking to the road
Yes, I'm taking to the rain
I'm taking to the snow
O my friend, my only brother
Do not let the party grieve
So throw a dollar onto the bar
Now kiss my ass and leave

O brother, my cup is empty
And I haven't got a penny
For to buy no more whiskey
I have to go home

Christina The Astonishing

Christina the Astonishing
Lived a long long time ago
She was stricken with a seizure
At the age of twenty-two
They took her body in a coffin
Just after the Agnus Dei
She soared up to the rafters
Perched on a beam up there
Cried, "The stink of human sin
Is more than I can bear"
Christina the Astonishing
Was the most astonishing of all
She prayed balanced on a hurdle
Or curled up into a ball
She fled to remote places
Climbed towers and trees and walls
To escape the stench of human corruption
Into an oven she did crawl
O Christina the Astonishing
Behaved in a terrifying way
She would run wildly through the streets
Jump in the Meusse and swim away
O Christina the Astonishing
Behaved in a terrifying way
Died at the age of seventy-four
In the convent of St. Anna

~~OVER HER DEAD BODY~~

OVER HER DEAD BODY

- ALFRED SCHNITTKE
- GABRIEL FAURÉ – REQUIEM
- SAMUEL BARBER **ADAGIO**
- ALBIONI – piece called ADAGIO
- TCHIAKOVSKY – VIOLIN CONCERTO in D
- FRITZ KREISLER – VIOLINIST anything by him

BARTOK ← String quartets BLUEBEARDS CASTLE

- LIGETI – LUX ETERNA (String Quartet)

STRAUSS – Metamorphosan

SORABJI (Altarus label)

LA CANTA DELLA SIBYLLA – Montserrat Figueras (Astrée label)

WERGO (great Mod. Classical Record Label)

When I First Came To Town

When I first came to town
All the people gathered round
They bought me drinks
Lord, how quickly they changed their tune

When I first came to town
People took me round from end to end
Like someone may take round a friend
O how quickly they changed their tune

Suspicion and dark murmurs surround me
Everywhere I go they confound me
As though the blood on my hands
Is there for every citizen to see

O sweet Jesus
There is no turning back
There is always one more town
A little further down the track

And from my window, across the tracks
I watch the juicers burn their fires
And in that light
Their faces leer at me
How I wish they'd just let me be

When I first came to town
Their favours were for free
Now even the doors of the whores of this town
Are closed to me

I search the mirror
And I try to see
Why the people of this town
Have washed their hands of me

O sweet Jesus
There is no turning back
There is always one more town
A little further down the track

O Lord, every God-damn turn I take
I fear the noose, I fear the stake
For there is no bone
They did not break
In all the towns I've been before

Well, those that sin against me are snuffed out
I know that from every day that I live
God-damn the day that I was born
The night that forced me from the womb
And God-damn this town
For I am leaving now
But one day I will return
And the people of this town will surely see
Just how quickly the tables turn

O sweet Jesus
This really is the end
There is always one more town
A little further round the bend

John Finn's Wife

Well, the night was deep and the night was dark
And I was at the old dance-hall on the edge of town
Some big ceremony was going down
Dancers writhed and squirmed and then
Came apart and then writhed again
Like squirming flies on a pin
In the heat and in the din
Yes, in the heat and in the din
I fell to thinking about the brand new wife of mad John Finn

Well, midnight came and a clock did strike
And in she came, did John Finn's wife
With legs like scissors and butcher's knives
A tattooed breast and flaming eyes
And a crimson carnation in her teeth
Carving her way through the dance floor
And I'm standing over by the bandstand
Every eye gaping on John Finn's wife
Yeah, every eye gaping on John Finn's wife

Now John Finn's wife was something of a mystery
In a town where to share a sworn secret was a solemn duty
I had brass knuckles and a bolo knife
Over near the bandstand with John Finn's wife
She got perfumed breasts and raven hair
Sprinkled with wedding confettis
And a gang of garrotters were all giving me stares
Armed, as they were, with machetes
And the night through the window was full of lights
Winking and a-watching at John Finn's wife

Next came the cops, all out on the town
But it don't look like no trouble there
As they had for the bar in their lumpy suits
And I slip my hand between the legs of John Finn's wife

And they seemed to yawn awake, her thighs
It was a warm and very ferocious night
The moon was full of blood and light
And my eyes grew small and my eyes grew tight
As I plotted in the ear of John Finn's wife

Enter John Finn in his shrunken suit
With his quick black eyes and black cheroot
With this filed-down teeth and a hobnail boot
And his fists full of pistols in his pockets
Aiming at me and aiming at his wife
The band fall silent fearing for their lives
And with fear in my guts like tangled twine
'Cause all I got is brass knuckles and a bolo knife
And mad John Finn's wife is all
And the three of us walk out of the hall

Now the night bore down upon us all
You could hear the crickets in the thickets call
And guns did flare and guns did bawl
And I planted my bolo knife in the neck
Of mad John Finn. I took his wretched life
Now I'm over by the bandstand
Every hand moving on John Finn's wife
Every hand moving on John Finn's wife

And John Finn's wife
Took all the flowers down from her hair
And threw them on the ground
And the flies did hum
And the flies did buzz around
Poor John Finn
Lying dead upon the ground
Lying dead upon the ground

The Loom Of The Land

It was the dirty end of winter
Along the loom of the land
When I walked with sweet Sally
Hand upon hand

And the wind it bit bitter
For a boy of no means
With no shoes on his feet
And a knife in his jeans

Along the loom of the land
The mission bells peeled
From the tower at Saint Mary's
Down to Reprobate Fields

And I saw that the world
Was all blessed and bright
And Sally breathed softly
In the majestic night

O baby, please don't cry
And try to keep
Your little head upon my shoulder
Now go to sleep

The elms and the poplars
Were turning their backs
Past the rumbling station
We followed the tracks

We found an untrodden path
And followed it down
The moon in the sky
Like a dislodged crown

My hands they burned
In the folds of her coat
Breathing milky white air
From deep in her throat

O baby, please don't cry
And try to keep
Your little head upon my shoulder
Now go to sleep

I told Sally in whispers
I'll never bring you harm
Her breast it was small
And warm in my palm

I told her the moon
Was a magical thing
That it shone gold in the winter
And silver in spring

And we walked and walked
Across the endless sands
Just me and my Sally
Along the loom of the land

O baby, please don't cry
And try to keep
Your little head upon my shoulder
Now go to sleep

Jack The Ripper

I got a woman
She rules my house with an iron fist
I got a woman
She rules my house with an iron fist
She screams out Jack the Ripper
Every time I try to give that girl a kiss

I got a woman
She strikes me down with a fist of lead
I got a woman
She strikes me down with a fist of lead
We bed in a bucket of butcher's knives
I awake with a hatchet hanging over my head

Well, you know the story of the viper
It's long and lean with a poison tooth
Yeah, you know the story of the viper
It's long and lean with a poison tooth
Well, they're hissing under the floorboards
Hanging down in bunches from my roof

I got a woman
She just hollers what she wants from where she is
I got a woman
She just hollers what she wants from where she's at
She screams out Jack the Ripper
Every time I try to give that girl a kiss

Cupid ~~Eros~~ is looking tired

We've looked at the All his arrows have been fired

And discovered And missed

I

~~And Eros is sick of waiting~~

~~And he is contemplating~~

~~Getting pissed~~ ~~have been throwing dice~~

~~The Gods [illegible]~~

At ~~[illegible]~~ ~~the gates of paradise~~

I

Saint Peter's so fucked off

that he has struck us off

his ~~the~~ list

"IN THE BEGINNING WAS THE WORD"

IN THRALL

SUCH A SMILE, BY SUCH A LOVER KISSED AWAY

At the CORE OF DESIRE is IMAGINATION

lakes of ink, millions of megabytes

THERE IS NO SUCH THING AS A MORAL BOOK OR AN IMMORAL BOOK

BOOKS ARE WELL WRITTEN OR BADLY WRITTEN THAT IS ALL. OSCAR WILDE

"KRUPTADIA" – PORNOGRAPHY

– CATCH A RED FISH WHICH LIES QUIVERING +

SPLENDID IN MY FINGERS.

THE BOAT OF HEAVEN – + CUNT.

Faraway, So Close!

Empty out your pockets, toss the lot upon the floor
All those treasures, my friend, you don't need them anymore
Your days are all through dying, they gave all their ghosts away
So kiss close all of your wounds and call living life a day

The planets gravitate around you
And the stars shower down around you
And the angels in Heaven adore you
And the saints they all stand and applaud you
So faraway, so faraway and yet so close

Say farewell to the passing of the years
Though all your sweet goodbyes will fall upon deaf ears
Kiss softly the mouths of the ones you love
Beneath the September moon and the heavens above

And the world will turn without you
And history will soon forget about you
But the heavens they will reward you
And the saints will all be there to escort you
So faraway, so faraway and yet so close

Do not grieve at the passing of mortality
For life's but a thing of terrible gravity
And the planets gravitate around you
And the stars shower down about you
And the angels in Heaven adore you
While those saints they all stand and applaud you
So faraway, so faraway and yet so close

Cassiel's Song

We've come to bring you home
Haven't we, Cassiel?

To cast aside your loss and all of your sadness
And shuffle off that mortal coil and mortal madness
For we're here to pick you up and bring you home
Aren't we, Cassiel?

It's a place where you did not belong
Where time itself was mad and far too strong
Where life leapt up laughing and hit you head on and hurt you
Didn't it hurt you, Cassiel?

While time outran you and trouble flew toward you
And you were there to greet it
Weren't you, foolish Cassiel?

But here we are, we've come to call you home
And here you'll stay, never more to stray
Where you can kick off your boots of clay
Can't you, Cassiel?

For death and you did recklessly collide
And time ran out of you, and you ran out of time
Didn't you, Cassiel?

And all the clocks in all the world
May this once just skip a beat in memory of you
But then again those damn clocks, they probably won't
Will they, Cassiel?

One moment you are there
Then strangely you are gone
But on behalf of us all here
We're glad to have you home
Aren't we, dear Cassiel?

Blue Bird

I got a blue bird
A blue bird on my shoulder
I got a blue bird
A blue bird on my shoulder

I saw her standing
Standing by the water
She was naked
Her hair in great disorder

And I know why I'm flying
And the rest is lies

I sent a warning
A warning of disaster
I sent a warning
I warned of great disaster

I sent that blue bird
That blue bird down the water
I sent that blue bird
Floating down the water

And I know that I'm flying
And the rest is lies

And I know that I'm flying
And the rest is lies

LET LOVE IN

Do You Love Me?
Nobody's Baby Now
Loverman
Jangling Jack
Red Right Hand
I Let Love In
Thirsty Dog
Ain't Gonna Rain Anymore
Lay Me Low
Do You Love Me? (Part 2)

Sail Away
Tread Softly (In Love)

Do You Love Me?

I found her on a night of fire and noise
Wild bells rang in a wild sky
I knew from that moment on
I'd love her 'til the day that I died
And I kissed away a thousand tears
My Lady of the Various Sorrows
Some begged, some borrowed, some stolen
Some kept safe for tomorrow
On an endless night, silver star-spangled
The bells from the chapel went jingle-jangle

Do you love me?
Do you love me?
Do you love me
Like I love you?

She was given to me to put things right
And I stacked all my accomplishments beside her
Still I seemed obsolete and small
I found God and all His Devils inside her
In my bed she cast the blizzard out
A mock sun blazed upon her head
So completely filled with light she was
Her shadow fanged and hairy and mad
Our love-lines grew hopelessly tangled
And the bells from the chapel went jingle-jangle

Do you love me?
Do you love me?
Do you love me
Like I love you?

She has a heartful of love and devotion
She had a mindful of tyranny and terror
Well, I try, I do, I really try
But I just err, baby, I do, I error

So come find me, my darling one
I'm down to the grounds, the very dregs
Ah, here she comes, blocking the sun
Blood running down the inside of her legs
The moon in the sky is battered and mangled
And the bells from the chapel go jingle-jangle

Do you love me?
Do you love me?
Do you love me
Like I love you?

All things move toward their end
I knew before I met her that I would lose her
I swear I made every effort to be good to her
I swear I made every effort not to abuse her
Crazy bracelets on her wrists and her ankles
And the bells from the chapel went jingle-jangle

Do you love me?
Do you love me?
Do you love me
Like I love you?

Nobody's Baby Now

I've searched the holy books
Tried to unravel the mystery of Jesus Christ the Saviour
I've read the poets and the analysts
Searched through the books on human behaviour
I travelled the whole world around
For an answer that refused to be found
I don't know why and I don't know how
But she's nobody's baby now

I loved her then and I guess I love her still
Hers is the face I see when a certain mood moves in
She lives in my blood and skin
Her wild feral stare, her dark hair
Her winter lips as cold as stone
Yeah, I was her man
But there are some things even love won't allow
I held her hand but I don't hold it now
I don't know why and I don't know how
But she's nobody's baby now

This is her dress that I loved best
With the blue quilted violets across the breast
And these are my many letters
Torn to pieces by her long-fingered hand
I was her cruel-hearted man
And though I've tried to lay her ghost down
She's moving through me, even now
I don't know why and I don't know how
But she's nobody's baby now

LOVER MAN

~~AND WE'D SIT IN THE PASTURE AND SAY~~
~~NOTHING COULD EVER GO WRONG~~

Let him in! Let him in! Let him in!

~~AND I'D SAY BUNNY LET'S GO TO BED~~
~~AND SHE'D LEAD ME WITH HER COLD HAND~~
~~I'D SAY I AM TIRED, I AM~~ I SAID

Loverman

There's a devil waiting outside your door
His eyes are dead + his heart is sore
A straining sex in his + a jumping paw
Yeah a devils waiting outside your door

I'll be your lover-man
forever, amen
Since the world began
~~A man loves a woman, a woman loves a man~~
~~Take off that dress~~ + I'll scream + I'll scream + I'll scream + I'll scream
I'll be your loverman
Cause I am what I am what I am what I
Take off that dress
Get on your knees
Lift up your hand . . . . ple-e-ease

LOVERMAN

There's a Devil waiting outside your door
(How much longer)
Bucking and braying and pawing at the floor
Well, he's howling with pain and crawling up the walls
There's a Devil waiting outside your door
He's weak with evil and broken by the world
He's shouting your name and asking for more
There's a devil waiting outside your door

Loverman! Since the world began
Forever, Amen 'til the end of time
Take off that dress, I'm coming down
I'm your Loverman!
'Cause I am what I am what I am what I am

L is for LOVE, baby
O is for ONLY you that I do
V is for loving VIRTUALLY everything that you are
E is for loving almost EVERYTHING that you do
R is for RAPE me
M is for MURDER me
A is for ANSWERING all of my prayers
N is for KNOWING your Loverman's going to be
the answer to all of yours

I'll be your Loverman 'til the bitter end
While empires burn down
Forever and ever and ever and ever, Amen
I'm your Loverman!
So help me, baby, so help me
'Cause I am what I am what I am what I am
I'm your Loverman!

There's a devil crawling along your floor
With a trembling heart, he's coming through your door
With his straining sex in his jumping paw
There's a devil crawling along your floor

And he's old and he's stupid and he's hungry and he's sore
And he's blind and he's lame and he's dirty and he's poor
There's a devil crawling along your floor

Loverman! Here I stand forever, Amen
'Cause I am what I am what I am what I am
Forgive me, baby, my hands are tied
And I got no choice, no, I got no choice at all

I'll say it again

L is for LOVE, baby
O is for O yes I do
V is for VIRTUE, so I ain't gonna hurt you
E is for EVEN if you want me to
R is for RENDER unto me, baby
M is for that which is MINE
A is for ANY old how, darling
N is for ANY old time

I'll be your Loverman! I got a masterplan
To take off your dress and be your man
Seize the throne, seize the mantle
Seize the crown
'Cause I am what I am what I am what I am
I'm your Loverman!

There's a devil lying by your side
You might think he's asleep but take a look at his eyes
He wants you, darling, to be his bride
There's a devil lying by your side

Loverman! Loverman!

Jangling Jack

Jangling Jack
Goes, "Yackety yack"
Visits the home of the brave
Hails a fat yellow cab
Jack wanna celebrate
Jack wanna big drink
Driver drops him at a bar
Called the Rinky Dink
Jack pushes through the door
And crosses the floor
Tips his hat to a man
Grinning in the corner
Going, "Do da do do da do"

Says, "I'm Jangling Jack
I go, 'Do do do'
I wanna Rinky Dink Special
I wanna little umbrella too"
Jack flops on his stool
Sees the grinning man laugh
So Jack laughs back
Jack raises his glass
Says, "God bless this country
And everything in it
The losers and the winners
The good guys and the sinners"
The grinning man says, "Buddy
It's all yackety yack"
Whips out a little black pistol
Shoots a bullet in Jack

Jangling Jack
Do da do do da do
Jangling Jack
How do you do da do

Jangling Jack flies off his seat
Crashes through the door
Lands in a heap on the street
Hears his mother's voice
Going, "Do do do"
Jack shouting
"Mummy, is that you?"
He sees the berserk city
Sees the dead stacked in piles
Sees the screaming crowd
Screams, "Where in Hell am I?"
Going, "Do da do"
Going, "Do da do"

Well, Jangling Jack
As a matter of fact
Crawls through the crowd
Back into the bar
Jack crawls to his stool
Jack drags himself up
Falls back down on his arse
In a puddle of blood
Going, "Goodbye, Mummy
Goodbye, goodbye"
Jack doubles over
And he vomits and dies
Going, "Do do do"
Going, "Do do do"

Red Right Hand

Take a little walk to the edge of town
Go across the tracks
Where the viaduct looms like a bird of doom
As it shifts and cracks
Where secrets lie in the border fires, in the humming wires
Hey man, you know you're never coming back
Past the square, past the bridge, past the mills, past the stacks
On a gathering storm comes a tall handsome man
In a dusty black coat with a red right hand

He'll wrap you in his arms, tell you that you've been a good boy
He'll rekindle all those dreams it took you a lifetime to destroy
He'll reach deep into the hole, heal your shrinking soul
Hey buddy, you know you're never ever coming back
He's a ghost, he's a god, he's a man, he's a guru
They're whispering his name across this disappearing land
But hidden in his coat is a red right hand

You ain't got no money? He'll get you some
You ain't got no car? He'll get you one
You ain't got no self-respect, you feel like an insect
Well, don't you worry, buddy, 'cause here he comes
Through the ghetto and the barrio and the bowery and the slum
A shadow is cast wherever he stands
Stacks of green paper in his red right hand

You'll see him in your nightmares, you'll see him in your dreams
He'll appear out of nowhere but he ain't what he seems
You'll see him in your head, on the TV screen
And hey buddy, I'm warning you to turn it off
He's a ghost, he's a god, he's a man, he's a guru
You're one microscopic cog in his catastrophic plan
Designed and directed by his red right hand

I Let Love In

Despair and Deception, Love's ugly little twins
Came a-knocking on my door, I let them in
Darling, you're the punishment for all my former sins

I let love in

The door it opened just a crack, but Love was shrewd and bold
My life flashed before my eyes, it was a horror to behold
A life-sentence sweeping confetti from the floor of a concrete hole

I let love in

Well, I've been bound and gagged and I've been terrorized
And I've been castrated and I've been lobotomized
But never has my tormentor come in such a cunning disguise

I let love in

O Lord, tell me what I done
Please don't leave me here on my own
Where are my friends?
My friends are gone

So if you're sitting all alone and hear a knocking at your door
And the air is full of promises, well buddy, you've been warned
Far worse to be Love's lover than the lover that Love has scorned

I let love in

Thirsty Dog

I know you've heard it all before
But I'm sorry for this three year war
For the setting up of camps and wire and trenches
I'm sorry for the other night
I know sorry don't make it right
I'm sorry for things I can't even mention

I'm sorry sorry sorry, sorry
I'm sitting feeling sorry in the Thirsty Dog
I'm sorry sorry sorry, sorry
I'm feeling very sorry in the Thirsty Dog

You keep nailing me back into my box
I'm sorry I keep popping back up
With my crazy mouth and jangling jester's cap
I'm sorry I ever wrote that book
I'm sorry about the way I look
But there ain't a lot that I can do about that

I'm sorry sorry sorry, sorry
I'm sitting feeling sorry in the Thirsty Dog
I'm sorry sorry sorry, sorry
I'm feeling sorry in the Thirsty Dog

I'm sorry about the hospital
Some things are unforgivable
Some things simply cannot be forgiven
I was not equipped to know how to care
And on the occasions I came up for air
I saw my life and wondered what the hell had I been living

I'm sorry sorry sorry, sorry
I'm sitting feeling sorry in the Thirsty Dog
I'm sorry sorry sorry, sorry
I'm sitting feeling sorry in the Thirsty Dog

I'm sorry about all your friends
I hope they'll speak to me again
I said before I'd pay for all the damage
I'm sorry it's just rotten luck
I'm sorry I've forgotten how to fuck
It's just that I think my heart and soul are kind of famished

I'm sorry sorry sorry, sorry
I'm sitting feeling sorry in the Thirsty Dog
I'm sorry sorry sorry, sorry
I'm feeling very sorry in the Thirsty Dog

Forgive me, darling, but don't worry
Love is always having to say you're sorry
And I am, from my head down to my shoes
I'm sorry that I'm always pissed
I'm sorry that I exist
And when I look into your eyes
I can see you're sorry too

I'm sorry sorry sorry, sorry
I'm sitting feeling sorry in the Thirsty Dog
I'm sorry sorry sorry, sorry
I'm feeling very sorry in the Thirsty Dog

Ain't Gonna Rain Anymore

Once there came a storm in the form of a girl
It blew to pieces my snug little world
And sometimes I swear I can still hear her howl
Down through the wreckage and the ruins

And it ain't gonna rain anymore
Now my baby's gone
And it ain't gonna rain anymore
Now my baby's gone

Now the storm has passed over me
I'm left to drift on a dead calm sea
And watch her forever through the cracks in the beams
Nailed across the doorways of the bedrooms of my dreams

And it ain't gonna rain anymore
Now my baby's gone
And it ain't gonna rain anymore
Now my baby's gone

Now I have no one to hold
Now I am all alone again
It ain't too hot and it ain't too cold
And there is no sign of rain

And it ain't gonna rain anymore
Now my baby's gone, yeah
And it ain't gonna rain anymore
Now my baby's gone, yeah
And I'm on my own

She ain't coming back no more
She ain't coming back no more
She ain't coming back no more
Say what you will, I don't care

Lay me low

CHORUS Lay me Low (chant)

Verses - same chords - but no chant
+ free-er lyrics

It's lonely at the top, jack

et + blizzard

w/ a word ~~song~~ and a kiss + a slam

SONG

they call me SUGAR-BOY bom bom

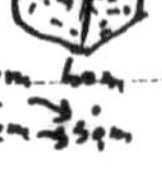

cause I'm white bom bom
+ I'm sweet bom bom
+ I melt bom bom
in the heat bom bom
bom bom

yeah sugar boy bum bom
sugar boy bom bom
I turn you on
+ I want you down here

Lay Me Low

They're gonna lay me low
They're gonna sink me in the snow
They're gonna throw back their heads and crow
When I go

They're gonna jump and shout
They're gonna wave their arms about
All the stories will come out
When I go

All the stars will glow bright
My friends will give up the fight
They'll see my work in a different light
When I go

They'll try telephoning my mother
They'll end up getting my brother
Who'll spill the story on some long-gone lover
I hardly know

Hats off to the man
On top of the world
Come crawl up here, baby
And I'll show you how it works
If you wanna be my friend
And you wanna repent
And you want it all to end
And you wanna know when
Then take a bow
Do it now, do it any old how
Make a stand, take my hand
And blow it all to Hell

They'll inform the police chief
Who will breathe a sigh of relief
He'll say I was a malanderer, a badlander and a thief
When I go

They will interview my teachers
Who'll say I was one of God's sorrier creatures
There'll be informative six-page features
When I go

They'll bang a big old gong
The motorcade will be ten miles long
The world will join together for a farewell song
When they put me down below

They'll sound a fluegelhorn
The sea will rage, the sky will storm
All man and beast will mourn
When I go

Hats off to the man
On top of the world
Crawl over here, darling
And we can watch this damn thing turn
If you wanna be my friend
And you wanna repent
And you want it all to end
And you wanna know when
Then do it now
Don't care how, do it any old how
Take my hand, make a stand
And blow it all to Hell

Do You Love me

A Song about everything
a big beautiful jumble of
words lurching onto Do you Love
me? chorus, ...

Do You Love Me? (Part 2)

Onward! And onward! And onward I go!
Where no man before could be bothered to go
'Til the soles of my shoes are shot full of holes
And it's all downhill with a bullet
This ramblin' and rovin' has taken its course
I'm grazing with the dinosaurs and the dear old horses
And the city streets crack and a great hole forces
Me down with my soapbox, my pulpit
The theatre ceiling is silver star-spangled
And the coins in my pocket go jingle-jangle

Do you love me?
Do you love me?
Do you love me?
Do you love me?

There's a man in the theatre with girlish eyes
Who's holding my childhood to ransom
On the screen there's a death, there's a rustle of cloth
And a sickly voice calling me handsome
There's a man in the theatre with sly girlish eyes
On the screen there's an ape, a gorilla
There's a groan, there's a cough, there's a rustle of cloth
And a voice that stinks of death and vanilla
This is a secret, mauled and mangled
And the coins in my pocket go jingle-jangle

Do you love me?
Do you love me?
Do you love me?
Do you love me?

The walls of the ceiling are painted in blood
The lights go down, the red curtains come apart
The room is full of smoke and dialogue I know by heart
And the coins in my pocket go jingle-jangle

As the great screen crackled and popped
The clock of my boyhood was wound down and stopped
And my handsome little body oddly propped
And my trousers right down to my ankles
Yes, it's onward! And upward!
And I'm off to find love
Do you love me? If you do, I'm thankful

Do you love me?
Do you love me?
Do you love me?
Do you love me?

This city is an ogre squatting by the river
It gives life but it takes it away, my youth
There comes a time when you just cannot deliver
This is a fact. This is a stone cold truth
Do you love me?
I love you, handsome
But do you love me?
Yes, I love you, you are handsome
Amongst the cogs and the wires, my youth
Vanilla breath and handsome apes with girlish eyes
Dreams that roam between truth and untruth
Memories that become monstrous lies
So onward! And onward! And onward I go!
Onward! And upward! And I'm off to find love
With blue-black bracelets on my wrists and ankles
And the coins in my pocket go jingle-jangle

Do you love me?
Do you love me?
Do you love me?
Do you love me?

Sail Away

I climbed the hill, lay in the grass
A little dark-eyed girl drifted past
She said, "All the best has come, it could not last
And the worst it has come true"

Her hands were small and fluttered up
A lamb amongst the buttercups
I pulled on my coat and buttoned it up
For the worst it had come true

Sail away, sail away
To a place where your troubles can't follow
Sail away, sail away
Save all your tears for tomorrow

The fins of the city moved toward us
And the swallows swooped and the starlings warned us
And the peril in everything it assured us
That the worst it had come true

And all my sorrows made their bed beside me
The shame, the disgrace and the brutality
And she whispered then, "Let laughter flee
For the worst it has come true"

Dry your tears, forget why we're here
Leave all your sorrows behind you
Never lose heart, all things must pass
To a place where your troubles can't find you

She came beside me, amongst my coat
Her breath was warm against my throat
We clung to each other so very close
For the worst it had come true

Sail away, sail away
To a place where your heart will not shame you
Take my hand, through this night without end
For the worst it has come to claim you

Sail away, sail away
To a place where your heart will not shame you
Take my hand, through this night without end
For the worst it has come to claim you

Tread Softly (In Love)

Tread softy in love
Around the traps and haunts
For some bodies are lonely
And gentle cries
Escape from their clothes
Saying
Hold on, hold on
Hold on, hold on
Forever goes so light on their time
Hold on, hold on
Forever on lonely time goes their night

Tread softly in love
And be kind for they will know
That you are not of them
But still they will show grace
For you have nothing
Saying
Hold on, hold on
Hold on, hold on
Forever goes so light on their time
Hold on, hold on
Forever on lonely time goes their night

Tread softly in love
Take care not to disturb them if you find them asleep
They have so little time
Before they must awaken
Do not weep
Hold on, hold on
Hold on, hold on
Forever goes so light on their time
Hold on, hold on
Forever on lonely time goes their night

MURDER BALLADS

Song of Joy
Henry Lee
Lovely Creature
Where the Wild Roses Grow
The Curse of Millhaven
The Kindness of Strangers
Crow Jane
O'Malley's Bar

There Is A Light
The Ballad of Robert Moore and Betty Coltraine
King Kong Kitchee Kitchee Ki-Mi-O / Treatment For A Film
Time Jesum Transeuntum Et Non Revertentum

O'MALLEY'S BAR

LOVELY creatures

TEN MURDER BALLADS BY NICK CAVE & THE BAD SEEDS

CROW JANE
LOVELY CREATURE
RED RIGHT HAND
WHERE THE WILD ROSES GROW
THE CURSE OF MILLHAVEN
O'MALLEY'S BAR
~~WHERE THE WILD ROSES GO~~
HENRY LEE
~~STAGGER LEE~~
DEATH IS NOT THE END
WILLOW GARDEN
KENG KONG KITCHEE
BALLAD OF ROBERT MOORE & BETTY COLTRA[illegible]
THE KINDNESS OF STRANGERS
STAGGER LEE

Song Of Joy

Have mercy on me, sir
Allow me to impose on you
I have no place to stay
And my bones are cold right through
I will tell you a story
Of a man and his family
And I swear that it is true

Ten years ago I met a girl named Joy
She was a sweet and happy thing
Her eyes were bright blue jewels
And we were married in the spring
I had no idea what happiness a little love could bring
Or what life had in store
But all things move toward their end
All things move toward their end
Of that you can be sure

La la la la la la la la la la
La la la la la la la la la la

Then one morning I awoke to find her weeping
And for many days to follow
She grew so sad and lonely
Became Joy in name only
Within her breast there launched an unnamed sorrow
And a dark and grim force set sail
Farewell happy fields
Where joy forever dwells
Hail horrors hail

Was it an act of contrition or some awful premonition
As if she saw into the heart of her final blood-soaked night
Those lunatic eyes, that hungry kitchen knife
Ah, I see, sir, that I have your attention!

Well, could it be?
How often I've asked that question
Well, then in quick succession
We had babies, one, two, three

We called them Hilda, Hattie and Holly
They were their mother's children
Their eyes were bright blue jewels
And they were quiet as a mouse
There was no laughter in the house
No, not from Hilda, Hattie or Holly
"No wonder," people said, "poor mother Joy's so melancholy"
Well, one night there came a visitor to our little home
I was visiting a sick friend
I was a doctor then
Joy and the girls were on their own

La la la la la la la la la la
La la la la la la la la la la

Joy had been bound with electrical tape
In her mouth a gag
She'd been stabbed repeatedly
And stuffed into a sleeping bag
In their very costs my girls were robbed of their lives
Method of murder much the same as my wife's
Method of murder much the same as my wife's
It was midnight when I arrived home
Said to the police on the telephone
Someone's taken four innocent lives

They never caught the man
He's still on the loose
It seems he has done many many more
Quotes John Milton on the walls in the victim's blood
The police are investigating at tremendous cost
In my house he wrote, *"Red right hand"*

That, I'm told, is from *Paradise Lost*
The wind round here gets wicked cold
But my story is nearly told
I fear the morning will bring quite a frost

And so I've left my home
I drift from land to land
I am upon your step and you are a family man
Outside the vultures wheel
The wolves howl, the serpents hiss
And to extend this small favour, friend
Would be the sum of earthly bliss
Do you reckon me a friend?
The sun to me is dark
And silent as the moon
Do you, sir, have a room?
Are you beckoning me in?

La la la la la la la la la la
La la la la la la la la la la
La la la la la la la la la la
La la la la la la la la la la

Henry Lee

Get down, get down, little Henry Lee
And stay all night with me
You won't find a girl in this damn world
That will compare with me
And the wind did howl and the wind did blow
La la la la la
La la la la lee
A little bird lit down on Henry Lee

I can't get down and I won't get down
And stay all night with thee
For the girl I have in that merry green land
I love far better than thee
And the wind did howl and the wind did blow
La la la la la
La la la la lee
A little bird lit down on Henry Lee

She leaned herself against a fence
Just for a kiss or two
And with a little pen-knife held in her hand
She plugged him through and through
And the wind did roar and the wind did moan
La la la la la
La la la la lee
A little bird lit down on Henry Lee

Come take him by his lily-white hands
Come take him by his feet
And throw him in this deep deep well
Which is more than one hundred feet
And the wind did howl and the wind did blow
La la la la la
La la la la lee
A little bird lit down on Henry Lee

Lie there, lie there, little Henry Lee
'Til the flesh drops from your bones
For the girl you have in that merry green land
Can wait forever for you to come home
And the wind did howl and the wind did moan
La la la la la
La la la la lee
A little bird lit down on Henry Lee

Lovely Creature

There she stands, this lovely creature
There she stands, there she stands
With her hair full of ribbons
And green gloves on her hands

So I asked this lovely creature
Yes, I asked. Yes, I asked
Would she walk with me a while
Through this night so fast

She took my hand, this lovely creature
"Yes," she said. "Yes," she said
"Yes, I'll walk with you a while"
It was a joyful man she led

Over hills, this lovely creature
Over mountains, over ranges
By great pyramids and sphinxs
We met drifters and strangers

O the sands, my lovely creature
And the mad, moaning winds
At night the deserts writhed
With diabolical things

Through the night, through the night
The wind lashed and it whipped me
When I got home, my lovely creature
She was no longer with me

Somewhere she lies, this lovely creature
Beneath the slow drifting sands
With her hair full of ribbons
And green gloves on her hands

WHERE THE WILD ROSES GROW

They call me The Wild Rose
But my name was Elisa Day
Why they call me it I do not know
For my name was Elisa Day

From the first day I saw her I knew that she was the one
As she stared in my eyes and smiled
For her lips were the colour of the roses
That grew down the river, all bloody and wild

When he knocked on my door and entered the room
My trembling subsided in his sure embrace
He would be my first man, and with a careful hand
He wiped at the tears that ran down my face

They call me The Wild Rose
But my name was Elisa Day
Why they call me it I do not know
For my name was Elisa Day

On the second day I brought her a flower
She was more beautiful than any woman I'd seen
I said, "Do you know where the wild roses grow
So sweet and scarlet and free?"

On the second day he came with a single red rose
Said, "Will you give me your loss and your sorrow?"
I nodded my head, as I lay on the bed
He said, "If I show you the roses, will you follow?"

They call me The Wild Rose
But my name was Elisa Day
Why they call me it I do not know
For my name was Elisa Day

On the third day he took me to the river
He showed me the roses and we kissed
And the last thing I heard was a muttered word
As he stood smiling above me with a rock in his fist

On the last day I took her where the wild roses grow
And she lay on the bank, the wind light as a thief
As I kissed her goodbye, I said, "All beauty must die"
And lent down and planted a rose between her teeth

They call me The Wild Rose
But my name was Elisa Day
Why they call me it I do not know
For my name was Elisa Day

THE BAD SEEDS WOULD LIKE TO OFFER THEIR
CONDOLENCES, TO THE FOLLOWING ~~[illegible]~~ 80 LOVELY CREATURES

JOHN O'MALLEY + HIS ([illegible]) WIFE + their daughter Stob dog

MARTHA O'MALLEY
SIOBHAN O'MALLEY
KATHLEEN CARPENTER
~~[illegible]~~
M.E. CAFFREY
HENRY DAVENPORT
VINCENT WEST
JERRY BELLOWS (POOR MARY'S FATHER)
RICHARD HOLMES
MRS. RICHARD HOLMES.
SEBASTIAN RICHARDSON
FRANCIS BROOKES

O'malleys (12)

THE TWENTY MINERS FROM NEWTOWN, NEAR BROKEN HILL N.S.W

(4) R.R.H
(1) Henry Lee
(1) Lovely Creature

FATHER + 3 GIRLS
JOY, HILDA HATTIE HOLLY MILTON

HENRY LEE

GREEN GLOVED GIRL

BILL BLAKE JNR

BIKO THE TERRIER.

JOE HANDYMAN

CLASS OF 20 CHILDREN from MILLHAVEN PRIMARY (INC. STINKY [illegible]) (JONES SLOER)

(56) +1

33 TENANTS OF BELLA VISTA RISE

MRS. COLGATE (1)

MARY BELLOWS

BUCKET OF BLOOD BARKEEP (2)

BILLY DILLY BROWN (1)

ELISA DAY A.K.A THE WILD ROSE

8 Victims
fix Biko the terrier

MR. FROGEYES
MR. WINGNUT
TATTOOED SAILOR
ROBERT MOORE (4)

80 MURDERERS
+1 DOG-BIKO

SONGS ARE
THESE ~~RECORDINGS~~ ARE
DEDICATED TO THE 100 LOVELY CREATURES
WHO GAVE THEIR LIVES IN ORDER
TO MAKE THIS RECORDING. ALSO TO ROBIN COOK (19 - 199)
AKA DEREK RAYMOND

The legendary
ENGLAND'S ~~MOST BRILLIANT~~ ~~MURDERER WHOSE WEAPON OF CHOICE~~
GREATEST CRIME WRITER
A WRITER/ THE TYPEWRITER WEAPON OF CHOICE
A MURDERER WHOSE WEAPON OF CHOICE
THE TYPEWRITER PROJECTED SOME OF THE MOST BRILLIANT.
HAUNTING DIGRESSIONS ON EVIL WE EVER READ

The Curse Of Millhaven

I live in a town called Millhaven
And it's small and it's mean and it's cold
But if you come around just as the sun goes down
You can watch the whole town turn to gold
It's around about then that I used to go a-roaming
Singing La la la la, la la la lie
All God's children, they all gotta die

My name is Loretta but I prefer Lottie
I'm closing in on my fifteenth year
And if you think you have seen a pair of eyes more green
Then you sure didn't see them round here
My hair is yellow and I'm always a-combing
La la la la, la la la lie
Mama often told me, we all have to die

You must have heard about the Curse of Millhaven
How last Christmas Bill Blake's little boy didn't come home
They found him next week in One Mile Creek
His head bashed in and his pockets full of stones
Well, just imagine the wailing and moaning
La la la la, la la la lie
Even little Billy Blake, he had to die

Then Professor O'Rye from Millhaven High
Found nailed to his door his prize-winning terrier
The next day the old fool brought little Biko to school
And we all had to watch as he buried her
His eulogy to Biko had all the tears a-flowing
La la la la, la la la lie
Even God's little creatures, they have to die

Our little town fell into a state of shock
A lot of people were saying things that made little sense
Then the next thing you know the head of Handyman Joe
Was found in the fountain of the Mayor's residence
Foul play can really get a small town going
La la la la, la la la lie
All God's children, all have to die

Then, in a cruel twist of fate, old Mrs Colgate
Was stabbed but the job was not complete
The last thing she said before the cops pronounced her dead
Was, "My killer is Loretta and she lives across the street!"
Twenty cops burst through my door without even phoning
La la la la, la la la lie
The young ones, the old ones, they all gotta die

Yes, it is I, Lottie, the Curse of Millhaven
I've struck horror in the heart of this town
Like my eyes ain't green and my hair ain't yellow
It's more like the other way around
I gotta a pretty little mouth underneath all the foaming
La la la la, la la la lie
Sooner or later we all gotta die

Since I was no bigger than a weavil they've been saying I was evil
That if "bad" was a boot then I'd fit it
That I'm a wicked young lady, but I've been trying hard lately
O fuck it! I'm a monster! I admit it!
It makes me so mad, my blood really starts a-going
La la la la, la la la lie
Mama always told me that we all gotta die

Yeah, I drowned the Blakey kid, stabbed Mrs Colgate, I admit
Did the handyman with his circular saw in his garden shed
But I never crucified little Biko, that was two junior high school psychos
Stinky Bohoon and his friend with the pumpkin-sized head
I'll sing to the lot, now you got me going
La la la la, la la la lie
All God's children have gotta die

There were all of the others, all our sisters and brothers
You assumed were accidents best forgotten
Recall the children who broke through the ice on Lake Tahoo?
Everyone assumed the "Warning" signs had followed them to the bottom
Well, they're underneath the house where I do quite a bit of stowing
La la la la, la la la lie
Even twenty little children, they had to die

And the fire of '91 that razed the Bella Vista slum
There was the biggest shit-fight this country's ever seen
Insurance companies ruined, landlords getting sued
All 'cause of a wee little girl with a can of gasoline
Those flames really roared when the wind started blowing
La la la la, la la la lie
Rich man, poor man, all got to die

Well, I confessed to all these crimes and then they put me on trial
I was laughing when they took me away
Off to the asylum in an old black Mariah
It ain't home, but you know, it's fucking better than jail
It ain't such a bad old place to have a home in
La la la la, la la la lie
All God's children, they all gotta die

Now I got shrinks that will not rest with their endless Rorschach tests
I keep telling them they're out to get me
They ask me if I feel remorse and I answer, "Why of course!
There is so much more I could have done if they'd let me!"
So it's Rorschach and Prozac and everything is groovy
Singing La la la la, la la la lie
All God's children have all gotta die
La la la la, la la la lie
I'm happy as a lark and everything is fine
Singing La la la la, la la la lie
Yeah, everything is groovy and everything is fine
Singing La la la la, la la la lie
All God's children, they all gotta die

The Kindness Of Strangers

They found Mary Bellows cuffed to the bed
With a rag in her mouth and a bullet in her head
O poor Mary Bellows

She'd grown up hungry, she'd grown up poor
So she left her home in Arkansas
O poor Mary Bellows

She wanted to see the deep blue sea
She drove across Tennessee
O poor Mary Bellows

She met a man along the way
He introduced himself as Richard Slade
O poor Mary Bellows

Poor Mary thought that she might die
When she saw the ocean for the first time
O poor Mary Bellows

She checked in to a cheap little place
Richard Slade carried in her old suitcase
O poor Mary Bellows

"I'm a good girl, sir," she said to him
"I couldn't possibly permit you in"
O poor Mary Bellows

Slade tipped his hat and winked his eye
And turned away without goodbye
O poor Mary Bellows

She sat on her bed and thought of home
With the sea breeze whistling, all alone
O poor Mary Bellows

In hope and loneliness she crossed the floor
And undid the latch on the front door
O poor Mary Bellows

They found her next day cuffed to the bed
A rag in her mouth and a bullet in her head
O poor Mary Bellows

So mothers keep your girls at home
Don't let them journey out alone
Tell them this world is full of danger
And to shun the company of strangers
O poor Mary Bellows
O poor Mary Bellows

Crow Jane

Crow Jane, Crow Jane, Crow Jane
Horrors in her head
That her tongue dare not name
Lived all alone by the river
The rolling rivers of pain
Crow Jane, Crow Jane, Crow Jane, ah hah huh

There is one shining eye on a hard-hat
Company closed down the mine
Winking on the waters they came
Twenty hard-hats, twenty eyes
In her clapboard shack
Just six foot by five
They killed all her whiskey
Poured their pistols dry
Crow Jane, Crow Jane, Crow Jane, ah hah huh

Seems you've remembered
How to sleep, how to sleep
The house dogs are in your turnips
And your yard dogs are running all over the streets
Crow Jane, Crow Jane, Crow Jane, ah hah huh

"O Mr Smith and Mr Wesson
Why you close up shop so late?"
"Just fitted out a girl who looked like a bird
Measured .32, .44, .38
Asked that gal which road she was taking
Said she was walking the road of hate
But she hopped on a coal-trolley up to New Haven
Population: 48"
Crow Jane, Crow Jane, Crow Jane, ah hah huh

Your guns are drunk and smoking
They have followed you to the gate
Laughing all the way back from the new town
Population, now: 28
Crow Jane, Crow Jane, Crow Jane, ah hah huh

O'Malley's Bar

I am tall and I am thin
Of an enviable height
And I've been known to be quite handsome
From a certain angel and in a certain light

Well, I entered into O'Malley's
Said, "O'Malley, I have a thirst"
O'Malley merely smiled at me
Said, "You wouldn't be the first"

I knocked on the bar and pointed
To a bottle on the shelf
And as O'Malley poured me out a drink
I sniffed and crossed myself

My hand decided that the time was nigh
And for a moment it slipped from view
And when it returned, it fairly burned
With confidence anew

Well, the thunder from my steely fist
Made all the glasses jangle
When I shot him, I was so handsome
It was the light, it was the angle

Huh! Hmmmmm

"Neighbours!" I cried. "Friends!" I screamed
I banged my fist upon the bar
"I bear no grudge against you!"
And my dick felt long and hard

"I am the man for which no God waits
For which the whole world yearns
I'm marked by darkness and by blood
And one thousand powder-burns"

Well, you know those fish with the swollen lips
That clean the ocean floor?
When I looked at poor O'Malley's wife
That is exactly what I saw

I jammed the barrel under her chin
And her face looked raw and vicious
Her head it landed in the sink
With all the dirty dishes

Her little daughter Siobhan
Pulled beers from dusk 'til dawn
And amongst the townfolk, she was a bit of a joke
But she pulled the best beers in town

I swooped magnificent upon her
As she sat shivering in her grief
Like the Madonna painted on the church-house wall
In whale's blood and banana leaf

Her throat it crumbled in my fist
And I spun heroically around
To see Caffrey rising from his chair
I shot that motherfucker down

Mmmmmmmmm, yeah yeah yeah

"I have no free will," I sang
As I flew about the murder
Mrs Richard Holmes, she screamed
You really should have heard her

I sang and I laughed, I howled and I wept
I panted like a pup
I blew a hole in Mrs Richard Holmes
And her husband, he stood up

And he screamed, "You are an evil man"
And I paused a while to wonder
"If I have no free will then how can I
Be morally culpable, I wonder"

I shot Richard Holmes in the stomach
And gingerly he sat down
And he whispered weirdly, "No offense"
And lay upon the ground

"None taken," I replied to him
With which he gave a little cough
With blazing wings I neatly aimed
And blew his head completely off

I've lived in this town for thirty years
And to no-one am I a stranger
And I put new bullets in my gun
Chamber upon chamber

And when I turned my gun on the bird-like Mr Brookes
I thought of Saint Francis and his sparrows
And as I shot down the youthful Richardson
It was Sebastian I thought of, and his arrows

Hhhhhhhhhhh
Mmmmmmmmm

I said, "I want to introduce myself
And I am glad that you all came"
And I leapt upon the bar
And shouted my name

Well, Jerry Bellows, he hugged his stool
Closed his eyes and shrugged and laughed
And with an ashtray as big as a fucking big brick
I split his head in half

His blood spilled across the bar
Like a steaming scarlet brook
And I knelt at its edge on the counter
Wiped the tears away and looked

Well, the light in there was blinding
Full of God and ghosts and truth
I smiled at Henry Davenport
Who made no attempt to move

Well, from the position I was standing
The strangest thing I ever saw
The bullet entered through the top of his chest
And blew his bowels out on the floor

Well, I floated down the counter
Showing no remorse
I shot a hole in Kathleen Carpenter
Recently divorced

But remorse I felt and remorse I had
It clung to every thing
From the raven hair upon my head
To the feathers on my wings

Remorse squeezed my hand in its fraudulent claw
With its golden hairless chest
And I glided through the bodies
And killed the fat man Vincent West

Who sat quietly in his chair
A man become a child
And I raised the gun up to his head
Executioner-style

He made no attempt to resist
So fat and dull and lazy
"Do you know I live in your street?" I cried
And he look at me as though I were crazy

"O," he said, "I had no idea"
And he grew as quiet as a mouse
And the roar of the pistol when it went off
Near blew the hat right off the house

Well, I caught my eye in the mirror
And gave it a long and loving inspection
"There stands some kind of man," I roared
And there did, in the reflection

My hair combed back like a raven's wing
My muscles hard and tight
And curling from the business end of my gun
Was a query-mark of cordite

Well, I spun to the left, I spun to the right
And I spun to the left again
"Fear me! Fear Me!"
But no one did 'cause they were dead

Huh! Hmmmmmmmm

And then there were the police sirens wailing
And a bull-horn squelched and blared
"Drop your weapon and come out
With your hands held in the air"

Well, I checked the chamber of my gun
Saw I had one final bullet left
My hand, it looked almost human
As I held it to my head

"Drop your weapon and come out!
Keep your hands above your head!"
Well, I had one long hard think about dying
And did exactly what they said

There must have been fifty cops out there
In a circle around O'Malley's bar
"Don't shoot," I cried. "I'm a man unarmed!"
So they put me in their car

And they sped me away from that terrible scene
And I glanced out of the window
Saw O'Malley's bar, saw the cops and the cars
And started counting on my fingers

Aaaaaaaaah one, aaaaaaaah two, aaaaaah three, aaaah four
O'Malley's bar, O'Malley's bar

There Is A Light

Hey there, Sugar, where ya gunna go
I'm going downtown, Daddy-O
What ya gunna do when you get there, girl?
I'm gunna get messed up in a God-shaped hole
Hey, Mr Hophead, what ya gunna do?
I'm going downtown for some bad ju-ju
Ya going downtown too, Mr Gigolo?
Damn right I am, Daddy-O

There is a light that shines over this city tonight
There is a light that shines over this city tonight
Let it shine

O Mr High-Roller, where you gunna go?
Where the real high-rolling rollers roll real dough
Hey, Mr Killer-Man, what you gunna do?
Me and Mr Death are going downtown too
Ain't there one God-fearing citizen about?
They're holed up and they ain't coming out
What about Mr Preacher to forgive our sins?
Not that carrion crow with blood on his chin
And Mr Politician, can't he lend a hand?
He's too busy sucking on the guts of this town
And what about God and this Armageddon?
He's all blissed-out, man, up in Heaven
Ain't there nowhere to run, ain't there nowhere to go?
Ain't there nowhere to run, ain't there nowhere to go?
Ain't there nowhere to run, ain't there nowhere to go?
Ain't there nowhere to run, ain't there nowhere to go?
Yeah, look to the sky, Daddy-O

There is a light that shines over this city tonight
There is a light that shines over this city tonight
Let it shine, let it shine, let it shine

What are the little kids gunna do, man?
The little kids are standing around
What are the kids doing, do you know?
They are looking to the sky, Daddy-O

The Ballad Of Robert Moore And Betty Coltraine

There was a thick-set man with frog-eyes was standing at the door
And a little bald man with wing-nut ears was waiting in the car
Well, Robert Moore passed the frog-eyed man as he walked into the bar
And Betty Coltraine she jumped under her table

"What's your pleasure?" asked the barman, he had a face like boiled meat
"There's a girl called Betty Coltraine that I have come to see"
"But I ain't seen that girl round here for more than a week"
And Betty Coltraine she hid beneath the table

Well, then in came a sailor with mermaids tattooed on his arms
Followed by the man with wing-nut ears who was waiting in the car
Well, Robert Moore sensed trouble, he'd seen it coming from afar
And Betty Coltraine she gasped beneath the table

Well, the sailor said, "I'm looking for my wife! They call her Betty Coltraine"
And the frog-eyed man said, "That can't be! That's my wife's maiden name!"
And the man with the wing-nut ears said, "Hey, I married her back in Spain"
And Betty Coltraine crossed herself beneath the table

Well, Robert Moore stepped up and said, "That woman is my wife"
And he drew a silver pistol and a wicked Bowie knife
And he shot the man with the wing-nut ears straight between the eyes
And Betty Cotlraine she moaned under the table

Well, the frog-eyed man jumped at Robert Moore who stabbed him in the chest
As Mr Frog-eyes died, he said, "Betty, you're the girl that I loved best"
Then the sailor pulled a razor and Robert blasted him to bits
And, "Betty, I know you're under the table!"

"Well, have no fear," said Robert Moore, "I do not want to hurt you
Never a woman did I love near half as much as you
You are the blessed sun to me, girl, and you are the sacred moon"
And Betty shot his legs out from under the table

Well, Robert Moore went down heavy with a crash upon the floor
And over to his thrashing body Betty Coltraine she did crawl
She put the gun to the back of his head and pulled the trigger once more
And blew his brains out all over the table

Well, Betty stood up and shook her head and waved the smoke away
Said, "I'm sorry, Mr Barman, to leave your place this way"
As she emptied out their wallets, she said, "I'll collect my severance pay"
Then she winked and threw a dollar on the table

King Kong Kitchee Kitchee Ki–Mi–O
Treatment For A Film

King Kong Kitchee Kitchee Ki-Mi-O is a rough translation of the traditional folk song, "Frog Went A-Courting."

> Mr Frog went a-courting and he did ride
> With a sword and a pistol by his side
> And he rode 'til he came to Miss Mouse's door
> And there he knelt down on the floor
> Kee-mo Kee-mo Kee-mo Kee
> He said, "Little Miss Mouse, will you marry me?"
> Way down yonder in a hollow tree
> With an own and a bat and a bumble bee
>
> Miss Mouse had suitors, three and four
> And they came rushing through the door
> Well, they grabbed Miss Mouse and began to fight
> In the hollow tree it was a terrible night
> "Little Miss Mouse, will you marry me?"
> Way down yonder in a hollow tree
> With an owl and a bat and a bumble bee
>
> Well, Mr Frog threw the suitors to the floor
> With his sword and his pistol he killed them all
> And they went to the vicar the very next day
> Then left on their honeymoon right away
> Glory glory glory be
> Way down yonder in a hollow tree
> With an owl and a bat and a bumble bee

The story is simple enough. The gallant Mr Frog sets out to court the nymphomaniacal Miss Mouse, "With a sword and a pistol by his side." He rides to her house. He proposes marriage. Miss Mouse has other suitors, who burst through the door and attempt to fight our stout-hearted frog. With his sword and his pistol, Mr Frog kills all four suitors. Awed by his martial spirit, Miss Mouse accompanies Mr Frog to the vicar, who marries them and together they leave on their honeymoon. The story takes place, "Way down yonder in a hollow tree / With an owl and a bat and a bumble bee," providing the evil ju-ju chant, "King Kong Kitchee Kitchee Ki-Mi-O."

This is the film:

In the beginning there is no music.

We see the front of a suburban home. We hear footsteps inside the house. A little yellow-haired girl opens the front door and hops down the steps into the dazzling sunlight.

She is a vision of childish beauty in yellow frock and yellow socks, with red ribbons in her pig-tails. She wears white gauze fairy wings. She is six. She opens the gate and steps out onto the footpath, looks briefly behind her and moves down the street. Her shiny black pumps clack as she walks. The camera follows her, observes her. Occasionally she stops to glance over her shoulder and the camera stops too. She continues a little more urgently. The camera moves after her. She stops at the corner, looks up and down the street, crosses the road, and enters a vacant lot. Again she looks behind her. She moves through the long dry grass. It crackles under her feet. The grass grows longer as she moves deeper into the lot. Her head is bent, she is looking at the ground. She stops, turns her head once more, then ducks down, out of view. The camera moves slowly, ominously, toward the spot where she disappeared.

It finds her. The little girl is squatting, her hand parting the grass in front of her. She glances once more at the camera, at us, then peers into the long grass she has opened with her hands. The camera, looming above her, follows her gaze, then moves past her. Deep into the grass. This is what we see:

In the North of Australia exists the massive cane-toad. These will be crudely animated, using real dead toads, to tell Mr Frog's story.

Down in this secret microcosm that the girl has exposed for us we see a little animal world in action.

The music begins.

Wearing tiny red trousers and a little hat sitting archly on his head, Mr Frog walks through a frog-sized forest. A miniature sword and pistol are tucked through his belt, a tiny bouquet in his hand.

Cane toads will play the voodoo chorus line, that of the owl, the bat and the bumble bee. The bumble bee will be a cane-toad dressed up like a bee, with little black and yellow striped t-shirt and fake springy antennae. The bat, a toad dressed in black with spooky vampire fangs, and the owl, a toad in brown feathery jacket with tiny granny glasses. These little toads will keep popping up when the change chimes in.

Anyway, off Mr Frog goes a-courting. He arrives at Miss Mouse's house and raps on the door. Miss Mouse, an actual rat, in low-cut sequined gown and tiny peroxided wig, ushers Mr Frog in.

Inside, on one knee, Mr Frog hands Miss Mouse the bouquet and proposes to her.

The door bursts open and in charge three toad-suitors, in trousers and hats. They leap at our bold Mr Frog, who draws his tiny sword and runs it through each suitor in turn. Then, drawing his pistol, he gives each of them a bullet in the back of the head for good measure. Miss Mouse flushes and swoons. Mr Frog is right there to catch her.

The scene changes to the couple leaving the house. Miss Mouse wears a lovely white wedding dress and veil. Mr Frog is dashing in his white tuxedo, his ever-present sword and pistol tucked into this trousers. They make their way back through the frog-sized forest.

"King Kong Kitchee Kitchee Ki-Mi-O," chant the kooky toad-owl, toad-bat and toad-bee.

Mr Frog and Miss Mouse arrive at a miniature chapel in a grove of cherry tress. The Vicar, a toad in a dog-collar with a tiny Bible, stands outside. He marries them. They kiss, as all the pink blossoms shower down around them like confetti.

The music ends.

A giant droplet of blood, in slow motion, splashes on Miss Mouse's head, drenching her veil. Mr Frog leaps back with his sword drawn, staring at the sky. He too is hit with blood, staining his tuxedo. Then more. Huge drops, in slow motion. A rain of blood comes down. Then slowly, falling from the sky, a giant red ribbon.

The screen turns black.

Time Jesum Transuentum Et Non Revertentum

We were called to the forest and we went down
A wind blew warm and eloquent
We were searching for the secrets of the universe
And we rounded up demons
And forced them to tell us what it all meant
We tied them to trees and broke them down one by one
On a scrap of paper they wrote these words
And as we read them the sun broke through the trees
"Dread the passage of Jesus for He will not return"
Then we headed back to our world and left the forest behind
Our hearts singing with all the knowledge of love
But somewhere, somehow we lost the message along the way
And when we got home we bought ourselves a house
And we bought a car that we did not use
And we bought a cage and two singing birds
And at night we'd sit and listen to the canaries' song
For we'd both run right out of words
Now the stars they are all angled wrong
And the sun and the moon refuse to burn
But I remember a message in a demon's hand
Dread the passage of Jesus for He does not return

~ MISERERE ~

"TIME JESUM TRANSEUTEM ET NON REVERTENTEM"

We were called to the forest. We went down.
~~It was dark, the air was full of~~ an alien light filled the air with ill portent
We fought for the secrets of the universe
We tied demons to trees, forced them to tell us what it meant
After many terrible days, we broke them all
On a scrap of paper they wrote these words
As we read them, our hearts swelled to burst
"DREAD THE PASSAGE OF JESUS, FOR HE WILL NOT RETURN."

We headed back to our world, left the forest behind.
Our hearts ~~clambering~~ singing with the knowledge of love
We lost the message along the way
When we got home we bought a house
We bought a car we did not use
We bought a cage and two singing birds
At night we'd listen to the canarys song
For we'd both run right out of words

Now the stars are all angled wrong
And both the sun and moon refuse to burn
And I remember a message in a demon's hand
"DREAD THE PASSAGE OF JESUS FOR HE DOES NOT RETURN"

DREAD THE PASSAGE OF JESUS FOR HE DOES NOT RETURN

DREAD THE PASSAGE OF JESUS FOR HE DOES NOT RETURN

DREAD THE PASSAGE OF JESUS FOR HE DOES NOT RETURN

THE FLESH MADE WORD

HUMILITY LET GOD DECIDE OUTCOME

Lilla

This year, next year, sometime, never.

Titus Andronicus, ______, + ... saying
'This is Literature' as if it were some closet vice.
So I grew up with the notion that to create, ~~to ex~~ was
a way to seperate oneself from normality. And it was. At school
my friends + I were openly chastised for being interested in the arts.
To create became an armour that kept the world away. At twenty years
I started reading the bible. I found the stories, from the Bible
calling to me from somewhere in my subconscious, from my
childhood + I found in the tough prose of the old testament
a perfect language, at once mysterious + familiar, ~~to express~~
~~to plunder~~ that could inform my own
ill-formed artistic endeavors. I found there the voice of
God and it was vitriolic, angry + merciless and that suited
me fine. My writing had grown weary + it was an incredible struggle to write anything ~~against~~ sadder more introspective
it is hard to loathe everything ~~my~~ sustained hatred is a painful work
feeling all the time. It ultimately is so (damn) tiring and in the eerie figure
business, I mean it's so tiring the man of Sorrows I felt
that moves through the Gospels,
I was given a chance to ~~reinvent~~ redefine my relationship
with the word. As a result my writing began to change, ~~as did~~ ~~God's voice and~~ The voice
~~the voice of God~~ ~~which~~ that spoke through me now was softer, sadder more introspective.
I then got it into my head to write a book which I
called And the Ass Saw the Angel. It has I felt
did. I said something about me as much as the central
character, a mute boy called E.E.

The Flesh Made Word

(For BBC Radio 3, July 1996)

Jesus said, "Wherever two or more are gathered together, I am in your midst." Jesus said this because wherever two or more are gathered there is a communion, there is language, there is imagination. There is God. God is a product of the creative imagination and God is that imagination taken flight.

As a child I believed that to use the imagination was wicked. I saw my imagination as a dark room with a large bolted door that housed all manner of shameful fantasies. I could almost hear my secret thoughts bumping and scratching behind the door, begging me in whispers to be let out. To be told. Back then I had no idea that those dark mutterings were coming from God. At eight years old I joined the choir in our local Anglican church and I attended services twice a week for the next four years but the God I heard preached about there seemed remote and alien and uncertain. So I sat in the stalls, in my crimson cassock, while rogue thoughts oozed beneath the bolted door of my imagination.

As I grew older and entered my teens, my now-deceased father decided it was time to pass on to his son certain information. Here I was thirteen years old and he would usher me into his study, lock the door and begin reciting great bloody slabs from Shakespeare's *Titus Andronicus*, or the murder scene from *Crime and Punishment,* or whole chapters from Nabokov's *Lolita.* My father would wave his arms about, then point at me and say, "This, my boy, is literature!" and I could tell by the way it empowered him that he felt he was passing on forbidden knowledge. I would sit and listen to all these mad words pouring from his mouth, happy to be invited into his strange, anomalous world. I would watch my father lose himself in the outpourings of his own creative energy and although he would have laughed at this notion, what my father was finding in his beloved literature was God. Literature elevated him, tore him from normality, lifted him out of the mediocre and brought him closer to the divine essence of things. I had no notion of that then, but I did see somewhere that art had the power to insulate me from the mundanity of the world, to protect me. So I set about writing some really bad poems.

At around fifteen years of age, my friends and I formed a rock band and I gave up writing really bad poems and started writing really bad songs instead, and these songs were very much influenced by whatever the book was that I was reading at the time.

After I matriculated I went to Art School and it was there I began to be interested in religious art, largely, I think, because it irritated my instructors, who thought I should be more concerned with contemporary art forms. I had pictures by Grunewald, Fra Angelico, El Greco, Tintoretto and so on plastered around the walls of my work-space and I found, almost to my surprise, that I recognised the biblical scenes depicted in these pictures, knew the key players and their stories, so I went out and bought myself a pocket Bible, the King James Version, opened it up at the first page and began to read it. I found the stories of the Bible calling to me from somewhere in my subconscious, planted there in the choir-boy days of my childhood. I was still writing songs for the band I was in and I soon found in the tough prose of the Old Testament a perfect language, at once mysterious and familiar, that not only reflected the state of mind I was in at the time but actively informed my artistic endeavors. I found there the voice of God and it was brutal and jealous and merciless. For every bilous notion I harboured about myself and the world, and there were a lot of those, there in the Old Testament was its equivalent leaping off the pages with its teeth bared. The God of the Old Testament seemed a cruel and rancorous God and I loved the way He would wipe out entire nations at a whim. I loved to read the Book of Job and marvelled over the vain, distrustful God who turned the life of His "perfect and upright" servant into a living hell. Job's friend Eliphaz observed, "Man is born unto trouble, as the sparks fly upward," and those words seemed to my horrid little mind about right. And why wouldn't man be born into trouble, living under the tyranny of such a God? So it was the feeling I got from the Old Testament, of a pitiful humanity suffering beneath a despotic God, that began to leak into my lyric writing. As a consequence my words blossomed with a nasty, new energy. My band, which was called The Birthday Party, was all heavy bludgeoning rhythms and revved-up, whacked-out guitars and all I had to do was walk on stage and open my mouth and let the curse of God roar through me. Floods, fire and frogs leapt out of my throat. To loosely paraphrase William Blake, "I myself did nothing. I just pointed a damning finger and let the holy spirit do the rest."

Though I had no notion of that then, God was talking not just to me but *through* me, and His breath stank. I was a conduit for a God that spoke in a language written in bile and puke. And for while that suited me fine.

After a few years The Birthday Party fell apart and by this time I had grown weary and my writing too and it was an incredible struggle to squeeze out much at all. I was sick and I was disgusted and my God was in a similar condition. It was hard work loathing everything all the time. All that sustained hatred was a painful and tiring business. I would climb onto the stage and look down at the twisted faces that roared and shook their fists at me in the gloom and all I felt was sick and sad. I decided it was high time I started reading a different book, so I closed the Old Testament and I opened up the New.

There, in those four wonderful prose poems, Matthew, Mark, Luke and John, I slowly reacquainted myself with the Jesus of my childhood, that eerie figure that moves through the Gospels, the Man of Sorrows, and it was through him that I was given a chance to redefine my relationship with the world. The voice that spoke through me now was softer, sadder, more introspective.

The more I read the Gospels, the more Christ called to my imagination, for His journey was, it seemed to me, just that, a flight of the imagination. Christ who called Himself both the Son of Man and the Son of God, as the occasion warranted, was exactly that — a man of flesh and blood, so in touch with the creative forces inside himself, so open to His brilliant, flame-like imagination, that He became the physical embodiment of that force, God. In Christ the spiritual blue-print was set so that we ourselves could become God-like.

There is that wonderful story in the Gospel of John where the scribes and Pharisees brought to Jesus a woman taken in adultery, and in an attempt to trap Him, asked if the woman should now be stoned under the law of Moses. Christ did not answer straight away but rather stopped down and with His finger wrote on the ground, as though He didn't hear them. The Pharisees persisted and after a time Christ lifted Himself up and answered, "He that is without sin among you, let him first cast a stone at her." And again He stooped down. For me, this seemingly distracted gesture, the stooping and the writing on the ground, is Christ accessing the God in Himself. Christ then delivers the line that disempowers His opponents —

and what an extraordinary remark it is — then stoops again to recommune with God. What Christ shows us here is that the creative imagination has the power to combat all enemies, that we are protected by the flow of our own inspiration.

Clearly what Jesus most despised, what He really railed against time and time again, were the forces that represented the established order of things, symbolised by the scribes and Pharisees — those dull, small-minded scholars of religious law who dogged His every move. Christ saw them as enemies of the imagination, who actively blocked the spiritual flight of the people and kept them bogged down with theological nit-picking, intellectualism and law. What was Christ's great bugbear, and what has sat like dung in the doorway of the Christian Church ever since, was the Pharisees' preoccupation with the law, in preference to the *logos*. Said St Paul to the Corinthians, "The letter killeth, but the spirit giveth life." So how can one be elevated spiritually if they are loaded up with the chains of religious jurisprudence? How can the imagination be told how to behave? How can inspiration or for that matter God be moral?

"Woe unto you, scribes and Pharisees, hypocrites," berates Christ in Matthews, "for ye shut up the Kingdom of Heaven against men." And further on He says, "Ye are like unto whited sepulchres, which indeed appear beautiful outward, but are within full of dead men's bones." This was the language of the Lord and it was lines like these, that were at once compassionate and venomous, that I found reverberating through my own words. Christ was forgiving, merciful and loving but He was after all the Son of the Old Testament God and His Father's blood still boiled in His veins. In creating His Son, God the Father had evolved. He had moved on. No longer was God's mercy reserved for elect nations and their kings, no longer were the divine rewards handed down to lords temporal and spiritual. Christ, the Son, came as an individual, the Word made flesh, to set right the misguided notions of His Father — or, as Paul wrote to the Corinthians, "God was in Christ reconciling the world to Himself." Christ came to right the wrongs of His Father. Christ, the man, who abhorred the concept of a spiritual elite, spoke to every man. He came with the gift of language, or love, of imagination. Said Jesus, the Gospel of John, "The words that I speak unto you, they are spirit and they are life," and it is these words, His language, the *logos,* that sings so eloquently and mysteriously from the Gospels. Christ is the imagination, at times terrible, irrational, incendiary and beautiful — in short, God-like.

And so, like Jesus, there is the blood of my father in me, and it was from him that I inherited, among other things, a love of literature, of words. And just as Christ was to His Father, I am a generation further on, and, if you'll forgive me, Dad, in evolutionary terms an advanced version. What my father always wanted to do was to write a book, and in that room where he used to take me and commune with me through the language of others, him giving and I receiving, was a desk which contained the beginnings of several aborted novels, all neatly, sadly, filed and titled. When I was about twelve my father asked, me, weirdly, what I had done to assist humanity. I had no idea what he was talking about but turned the question around and asked him what *he* had done. He said he had written a couple of short stories that had been published in magazines and I shared in his pride as he showed them to me. But I noticed that the magazines were of an earlier decade and it was clear that these two short stories were tiny seeds planted in a garden that did not grow.

In 1985, I went to live in Berlin, where I got it into my head to write a novel, and for the next three years I locked myself away in a room in Kruezberg and wrote it. I called in *And the Ass Saw the Angel.* It was about a mad, hermetic mute boy called Euchrid Eucrow, who, having been denied the faculty of speech, eventually explodes in a catharsis of rage and brings to its knees the religious community in which he lives. The story, set in the American South and told through the voice or non-voice of Euchrid Eucrow, was written in a kind of hyper-poetic thought-speak, not mean to be spoken — a mongrel language that was part-Biblical, part-Deep South dialect, part-gutter slang, at times obscenely reverent and at others reverently obscene. Throughout the story, God fills the mute boy with information, loads him up with bad ideas, "hate inspiration straight from God," as he calls it, but with no one to talk to and no way to talk, Euchrid, like a blocked pipe, bursts. For me, Euchrid is Jesus struck dumb, he is the blocked artist, he is internalised imagination become madness.

God is not found *in* Christ, but *through* Him. In the Gospel of Thomas, the Gnostic scripture discovered at Nag Hammadi in Egypt in 1945, Christ states that "the kingdom is inside of you and it is outside of you." This statement must have terrified early Christian ministry as it rendered them obsolete — why do we need the church to bring us close to God when He already lives within us? — and hence the Nicene Council's decision not to allow it into the New Testament canon. Apart from the sheer subversiveness of this statement, what is really so remarkable about it is the emphasis it places upon our individual selves. Rather than praising a personal and supernatural God as an all-mighty, all-knowing, all-seeing force existing somewhere in the great beyond, the emphasis is placed clearly on man, that without him as a channel God has nowhere to go.

"Wherever two or more are gathered together, I am in your midst," Jesus said. Just as we are divine creations, so must we in turn create. Divinity must be given its freedom to flow, through us, through language, through communication, through imagination. I believe this is our spiritual duty made clear to us through the example of Christ. Through us God finds His voice, for just as we need God, He in turn needs us. God found life through my father as he raved and flailed about his study reciting his favorite literature, but died in the desk drawer that contained those pages, the first painful contractions of his stillborn dreams. My father asked me what I had done to assist humanity and at twelve years old I could not answer. I now know. Like Christ, I too come in the name of my father, to keep God alive.

THE BOATMAN'S CALL

Into My arms
Lime-Tree Arbour
People Ain't No Good
Brompton Oratory
There Is A Kingdom
(Are You) The One That I've Been Waiting For?
Where Do we Go Now But Nowhere?
West Country Girl
Black Hair
Idiot Prayer
Far From Me
Green Eyes

Wife
Little Empty Boat
Come Into My Sleep
Right Now, I Am A-Roamin'
Babe, I Got You Bad
The Bridle Path
Opium Tea
The Sweetest Embrace

Into My Arms

I don't believe in an interventionist God
But I know, darling, that you do
But if I did I would kneel down and ask Him
Not to intervene when it came to you
Not to touch a hair on your head
To leave you as your are
And if He felt He had to direct you
Then direct you into my arms

Into my arms, O Lord
Into my arms, O Lord
Into my arms, O Lord
Into my arms

And I don't believe in the existence of angels
But looking at you I wonder if that's true
But if I did I would summon them together
And ask them to watch over you
To each burn a candle for you
To make bright and clear your path
And to walk, like Christ, in grace and love
And guide you into my arms

Into my arms, O Lord
Into my arms, O Lord
Into my arms, O Lord
Into my arms

But I believe in Love
And I know that you do too
And I believe in some kind of path
That we can walk down, me and you
So keep your candles burning
And make her journey bright and pure
That she will keep returning
Always and evermore

Into my arms, O Lord
Into my arms, O Lord
Into my arms, O Lord
Into my arms

Lime–Tree Arbour

The boatman calls from the lake
A lone loon dives upon the water
I put my hand over hers
Down in the lime-tree arbour

The wind in the trees is whispering
Whispering low that I love her
She puts her hand over mine
Down in the lime-tree arbour

Through every breath that I breathe
And every place I go
There is a hand that protects me
And I do love her so

There will always be suffering
It flows through life like water
I put my hand over hers
Down in the lime-tree arbour

The boatman he has gone
And the loons have flown for cover
She puts her hand over mine
Down in the lime-tree arbour

Through every word that I speak
And every thing I know
There is a hand that protects me
And I do love her so

People Ain't No Good

People just ain't no good
I think that's well understood
You can see it everywhere you look
People just ain't no good

We were married under cherry tress
Under blossom we made our vows
All the blossoms come sailing down
Through these streets and through the playgrounds

The sun would stream on the sheets
Awoken by the morning bird
We'd buy the Sunday newspapers
And never read a single word

People they ain't no good
People they ain't no good
People they ain't no good

Seasons came, seasons went
The winter stripped the blossoms bare
A different tree now lines the street
Shaking its fists in the air

The winter slammed us like a fist
The windows rattling in the gales
To which she drew the curtains
Made out of her wedding veils

People they ain't no good
People they ain't no good
People they ain't no good

To our love send a dozen white lilies
To our love send a coffin of wood
To our love let all the pink-eyed pigeons coo
That people they just ain't no good
To our love send back all the letters

To our love a valentine of blood
To our love let all the jilted lovers cry
That people they just ain't no good

It ain't that in their hearts they're bad
They can comfort you, some even try
They nurse you when you're ill of health
They bury you when you go and die
It ain't that in their hearts they're bad
They'd stick by you if they could
But that's just bullshit
People they ain't no good

People they ain't no good
People they ain't no good
People they ain't no good
People they ain't no good

Brompton Oratory

Up those stone steps I climb
Hail this joyful day's return
Into its great shadowed vault I go
Hail the Pentecostal morn

The reading is from Luke 24
Where Christ returns to his loved ones
I look at the stone apostles
Think that it's alright for some

And I wish that I was made of stone
So that I would not have to see
A beauty impossible to define
A beauty impossible to believe

A beauty impossible to endure
The blood imparted in little sips
The smell of you still on my hands
As I bring the cup up to my lips

No God up in the sky
No Devil beneath the sea
Could do the job that you did
Of bringing me to my knees

Outside I sit on the stone steps
With nothing much to do
Forlorn and exhausted, baby
By the absence of you

There Is A Kingdom

Just like a bird that sings up the sun
In a dawn so very dark
Such is my faith for you
Such is my faith
And all the world's darkness can't swallow up
A single spark
Such is my love for you
Such is my love

There is a kingdom
There is a king
And He lives without
And He lives within

The starry heavens above me
The moral law within
So the world appears
So the world appears
This day so sweet
It will never come again
So the world appears
Through this mist of tears

There is a kingdom
There is a king
And He lives without
And He lives within
And He is everything

~~ONCE I HH~~

I HAVE A DOG. HE'S CALLED "SUCCESS"
FOLLOWS ME WHEREVER I RUN
SOMETIMES I CALL HIM "FAILURE"
~~HE~~ ANSWERS TO EITHER ONE.

throng
along
gong
long wrong
string
belong

O we will know ... Wont we?
will the ~~birds~~ animals burst into song ... when we kiss?
Will our words ~~all seem~~ come out all wrong ... when we ~~remember~~ kiss
Will the wind blow wild + strong .. is there rest for the wicked
O no there is not

R M L F
HIS & RES REST TRYST

Will the moon burn red hot .. when we touch
Will the planet slow down + stop .. as we catch
. the tears that fall ~~from~~ from our eyes
will we ever realise ... + if we do

O WE WILL KNOW .. WONT WE?
WILL THE STARS ALL EXPLODE IN THE SKY when we kiss
O WE KNOW .. DONT WE
IT'S THERE IN THE TEAR IN YOUR EYE

~~DO~~ WE TRY? DONT we?
O ~~WE DO, DONT WE~~.

that stars just shine for a ~~short~~ while then disappear

abyss

• THE GREAT CODE •
NORTHROPE FRYE

Will the pretty birds all start to sing .. when we kiss
Will all the bells of the city ring .. thru the mist ~~when we kiss~~
Will the children dress in flowers + bring bottles of bliss

(Are You) The One That I've Been Waiting For?

I've felt you coming, girl, as you drew near
I knew you'd find me, 'cause I longed you here
Are you my destiny? Is this how you'll appear?
Wrapped in a coat with tears in your eyes?
Well take that coat, babe, and throw it on the floor
Are you the one that I've been waiting for?

As you've been moving surely toward me
My soul has comforted and assured me
That in time my heart it will reward me
And that all will be revealed
So I've sat and I've watched an ice-age thaw
Are you the one that I've been waiting for?

Out of sorrow entire worlds have been built
Out of longing great wonders have been willed
They're only little tears, darling, let them spill
And lay your head upon my shoulder
Outside my window the world has gone to war
Are you the one that I've been waiting for?

O we will know, won't we?
The stars will explode in the sky
O but they don't, do they?
Stars have their moment and then they die

There's a man who spoke wonders though I've never met him
He said, "He who seeks finds and who knocks will be let in"
I think of you in motion and just how close you are getting
And how every little thing anticipates you
All down my veins my heart-strings call
Are you the one that I've been waiting for?

Where Do We Go Now But Nowhere?

I remember a girl so very well
The carnival drums all mad in the air
Grim reapers and skeletons and a missionary bell
O where do we go now but nowhere

In a colonial hotel we fucked up the sun
And then we fucked it down again
Well, the sun comes up and the sun goes down
Going round and around to nowhere

The kitten that padded and purred on my lap
Now swipes at my face with the paw of a bear
I turn the other cheek and you lay into that
O where do we go now but nowhere

O wake up, my love, my lover, wake up
O wake up, my love, my lover, wake up

Across clinical benches with nothing to talk
Breathing tea and biscuits and the Serenity Prayer
While the bones of our child crumble like chalk
O where do we go now but nowhere

I remember a girl so bold and so bright
Loose-limbed and laughing and brazen and bare
Sits gnawing her knuckles in the chemical light
O where do we go now but nowhere

You come for me now with a cake that you've made
Ravaged avenger with a clip in your hair
Full of glass and bleach and my old razor blades
O where do we go now but nowhere

O wake up, my love, my lover, wake up
O wake up, my love, my lover, wake up

If they'd give me my clothes back then I could go home
From this fresh, this clean, antiseptic air
Behind the locked gates an old donkey moans
O where do we go now but nowhere

Around the duck pond we grimly mope
Gloomily and mournfully we go round again
And one more doomed time and without much hope
Going round and around to nowhere

From the balcony we watched the carnival band
The crack of the drum a little child did scare
I can still feel his tiny fingers pressed in my hand
O where do we go now but nowhere

If I could relive one day of my life
If I could relive just a single one
You on the balcony, my future wife
O who could have known, but no one

O wake up, my love, my lover, wake up
O wake up, my love, my lover, wake up

West Country Girl

With a crooked smile and a heart-shaped face
Comes from the West Country where the birds sing bass
She's got a house-big heart where we all live
And plead and counsel and forgive
Her widow's peak, her lips I've kissed
Her glove of bones at her wrist
That I have held in my hand
Her Spanish fly and her monkey gland
Her Godly body and its fourteen stations
That I have embraced, her palpitations
Her unborn baby crying, "Mummy"
Amongst the rubble of her body
Her lovely lidded eyes I've sipped
Her fingernails, all pink and chipped
Her accent which I'm told is "broad"
That I have heard and has been poured
Into my human heart and filled me
With love, up to the brim, and killed me
And rebuilt me back anew
With something to look forward to
Well, who could ask much more than that?
A West Country girl with a big fat cat
That looks into her eyes of green
And meows, "He loves you," then meows again

Black Hair

Last night my kisses were banked in black hair
And in my bed, my lover, her hair was midnight black
And all her mystery dwelled within her black hair
And her black hair framed a happy heart-shaped face
And heavy-hooded eyes inside her black hair
Shined at me from the depths of her hair of deepest black
While my fingers pushed into her straight black hair
Pulling her black hair back from her happy heart-shaped face
To kiss her milk-white throat, a dark curtain of black hair
Smothered me, my lover with her beautiful black hair
The smell of it is heavy. It is charged with life
On my fingers the smell of her deep black hair
Full of all my whispered words, her black hair
And wet with tears and goodbyes, her hair of deepest black
All my tears cried against her milk-white throat
Hidden behind the curtain of her beautiful black hair
As deep as ink and black, black as the deepest sea
The smell of her black hair upon my pillow
Where her head and all its black hair did rest
Today she took a train to the West
Today she took a train to the West
Today she took a train to the West

BLACK HAIR

Last night my kisses were banked on black hair

In my bed, my lover her hair was midnite black

her essense, her mystery lives deep within her black hair

black hair that framed a heart-shaped face

And heavy hooded eyes so green inside her black hair

Looked at me from the depths of her hair of black

My fingers pushed + curled into her straight black hair

Pulling her hair of black back from her heart-shaped face

kiss her milk White throat. A dark curtain of black hair

which smothers me, my lover with the black hair

The smell of it is heavy. It is charged with life

On my fingers the smell of her deep black hair

As deep as ink + black as the deepest sea

smell. Her black hair. On my pillow

Where her head + all her hair did rest

Today she took a train + rode with it out West

Took a train + rode with it out West

Took a train + rode with it West.

(X2)

Idiot Prayer

They're taking me down, my friend
And as they usher me off to my end
Will I bid you adieu?
Or will I be seeing you soon?
If what they say around here is true
Then we'll meet again
Me and you

My time is at hand, my dove
They're gunna pass me to that house above
Is Heaven just for victims, dear?
Where only those in pain go?
Well, it takes two to tango
We will meet again, my love
I know

If you're in Heaven, then you'll forgive me, dear
Because that's what they do up there
But if you're in Hell, then what can I say
You probably deserved it anyway
I guess I'm gunna find out any day
For we will meet again
And there'll be Hell to pay

Your face comes to me from the depths, dear
Your silent mouth mouths, "Yes," dear
Dark red and big with blood
They're gunna shut me down, my love
They're gunna launch me into the stars
Well, all things come to pass
Yeah, Glory Hallelujah

This prayer is for you, my love
Sent on the wings of a dove
An idiot prayer of empty words
Love, dear, is strictly for the birds
We each get what we deserve
My little snow white dove
Rest assured

Far From Me

For you, dear, I was born
For you I was raised up
For you I've lived and for you I will die
For you I am dying now
You were my mad little lover
In a world where everybody fucks everybody else over
You who are so
Far from me
So far from me
Way across some cold neurotic sea
Far from me

I would talk to you of all manner of things
With a smile you would reply
Then the sun would leave your pretty face
And you'd retreat from the front of your eyes
I keep hearing that you're doing your best
I hope your heart beats happy in your infant breast
You are so far from me
Far from me
Far from me

There is no knowledge but I know it
There's nothing to learn from that vacant voice
That sails to me across the line
From the ridiculous to the sublime
It's good to hear you're doing so well
But really, can't you find somebody else that you can ring and tell?
Did you ever care for me?
Were you ever there for me?
So far from me

You told me you'd stick by me
Through the thick and through the thin
Those were your very words
My fair-weather friend
You were my brave-hearted lover
At the first taste of trouble went running back to mother
So far from me
Far from me
Suspended in your bleak and fishless sea
Far from me
Far from me

Green Eyes

Kiss me again, re-kiss me and kiss me
Slip your frigid hands beneath my shirt
This useless old fucker with his twinkling cunt
Doesn't care if he gets hurt

Green eyes, green eyes
Green eyes, green eyes

If it were but a matter of faith
If it were measured in petitions and prayer
She would materialise, all fleshed out
But it is not, nor do I care

Green eyes, green eyes
Green eyes, green eyes

So hold me and hold me, don't tell me your name
This morning will be wiser than this evening is
Then leave me to my enemied dreams
And be quiet as you are leaving, Miss

Green eyes, green eyes
Green eyes, green eyes

I spun heroic stories of great misery
Under a big green + red umbrella
You leaned ~~against~~ across the table + kissed me
~~Kids~~ whistling at us from the favela
children
I feel our planet about to collide
She is born to the ~~heart~~ ~~of~~ ~~her~~ bride
she is like kiss... the kiss of...
she is L.A.'s pride

Under a punishing sun
Under a big red + green umbrella
~~My ever-loving woman~~ beat the drums
Call her name + at her
~~Children whooping + whistling from the favela~~
Rolling down the hill from the favela
From the ocean up to the ~~favelas~~
outside bride guide
tied outside ~~died~~ side

cages / pages / rages / sages fool

Latin America's pride
has surrendered
God is dead yet we live on
She is the desire of the ages
History eternal woman
pages
The fire that leaps from
the Golden Bough's
Solomon's
not trap in
crosses or cages
we must find a new one
Not lock him down in cathedrals, or cages
I am searching for the eternal woman
the fire that leapt from Solomon's page up

God has lost
has you missing
DESERTED
She is Latin America's pride
God has deserted
yet we live on
We must not lock our gods
up in cages
heatless

P.3 (2) ~~3~~-365-52-12

~~[illegible]~~

12-52-365

Under a punishing sun
Under a red and green umbrella
Call her name and beat the drums
From the condominiums to the
~~Rolling down the hillside from the favelas~~
God is gone. We ~~must find~~ gotta get a new one
~~She is the desire of the ages~~
And not lock him down in cathedrals + cages
I searched + found the eternal woman
The fire that leapt up from Solomon's page
~~Oh baby here she comes~~
~~bride~~
~~She is the kiss of life to an ailing continent~~
~~Continent~~
Oh, baby, here she comes
My ~~wild restless~~ righteous ringless bride
She's ~~is~~ the ~~kiss of life to~~ soul of an ailing continent
~~(country)~~
She is Latin America's pride
There she goes, through the slum
Through cities of packed dirt + powdered bone
~~She belongs to you + [illegible] everyone~~
~~She is given unto you~~
She's ~~[illegible]~~ prepared to accept the burden of the world's great pain
Provide you accept the burden of your own

Wife

Here she comes, my wife
See her down on the street
Well, yeah, she's mine, supine
Or up on her feet

Yeah, here she comes
Through the dog-breath heat
With her concertina spine
And her ballerina feet

Under a punishing sun
Under a red and green umbrella
Call her name and beat the drum
Through the condominiums and the favelas

God is gone. We got to get a new one
Not lock Him down in cathedrals and cages
I found the eternal woman
The fire that leapt from Solomon's pages

O baby, here she comes
My righteous, ringless bride
She is the soul of an ailing continent
She is Latin America's pride

There she runs, through the rain
Through cities of packed dirt and bone
She's prepared to accept the burden of the world's great pain
Provided you accept the burden of your own

Ah, here she comes
I will love her for all time
In her little, small floral skirt, so short
Defying rhythm, defying rhyme

The cats are crying like babies
Up and down the alleys
The kids are howling like cats
With not enough in their bellies

Here, she's gaily tripping through the streets
Cats and kids stop to stare
The kids all band their guitars
They shoot their guns into the air

She don't carry no gun
Her lips are loaded up with kisses
She got kisses all around her hips
She got them criss-crossing her breasts

Keep playing that song
Don't let the band go home
I tell you God is gone
We are on our own

Yeah, here she comes
In a dress of red and yellow
Up the steps to our home
I got something to tell her

I say, I say, b-b-b-b-b-baby!
Ye-e-e-e-ah! Yea-a-a-a-h! Uh-huh!
O b-b-b-baby!
A-a-a-ah here she comes!

Little Empty Boat

You found me at some party
You thought I'd understand
You barrelled over to me
With a drink in each hand
I respect your beliefs, girl
And I consider you a friend
But I've already been born once
I don't wanna be born again
Your knowledge is impressive
And your argument is good
But I am the resurrection, babe
And you're standing on my foot

But my little boat is empty
It don't go!
And my oar is broken
It don't row, row, row!
My little boat is empty
It don't go!
And my oar is broken
It don't row, row, row!

Your tiny little face
Keeps yapping in the gloom
Seven steps behind me
With your dustpan and broom
I can't help but imagine you
All postured and prone
But there's a little guy on my shoulder
Says I should go home alone
But you keep leaning in on me
And you're looking pretty pissed
That grave you've dug between your legs
Is hard to resist

But my little boat is empty
It don't go!
And my oar is broken
It don't row, row, row!

My little boat is empty
It don't go!
And my oar is broken
It don't row, row, row!

Give to God what belongs to God
And give the rest to me
Tell our gracious host to fuck himself
It's time for us to leave

But my little boat is empty
It don't go!
And my oar is broken
It don't row, row, row!
My little boat is empty
It don't go!
And my oar is broken
It don't row, row, row!

Come Into My Sleep

Now that mountains of meaningless words
And oceans divide us
And we each have our own set of stars
To comfort and guide us
Come into my sleep
Come into my sleep
Dry your eyes and do not weep
Come into my sleep

Swim to me through the deep blue sea
Upon the scattered stars set sail
Fly to me through this love-lit night
From one thousand miles away
And come into my sleep
Come into my sleep
As midnight nears and shadows creep
Come into my sleep

Bind my dreams up in your tangled hair
For I am sick at heart, my dear
Bind my dreams up in your tangled hair
For all sorrow it will pass, my dear

Take your accusations, your recriminations
And toss them into the ocean blue
Leave your regrets and impossible longings
And scatter them across the sky behind you
And come into my sleep
Come into my sleep
For my soul to comfort and keep
Come into my sleep
Dry your eyes and come into my sleep

Right Now, I Am A-Roamin'

When I get home
I'm gunna clean up my house
When I get home
I'm gunna kick out that mouse
When I get home
I'm gunna put things in order
But right now, right right now
Right now, I am a-roamin'

When I get home
I'm gunna make that call
When I get home
I'm gunna talk it through
When I get home
I'm gunna straighten it out
But right now, right now
Right now, I am a-roamin'

When I get home
I'm gunna give up the booze
When I get home
I'm gunna eat some food
When I get home
I'm gunna kick them drugs
But right now, right now
Right now, I am a-roamin'

When I get home
I'm gunna call my mother
When I get home
I'm gunna cook her some dinner
When I get home
I'm gunna invite my brothers
But right now, right right now
Right now, I am a-roamin'

When I get home
I'm gunna see my little boy
When I get home

RIGHT NOW I AM A-ROAMING

WHEN I GET HOME
SEE MY LITTLE BOY
BRING HIM A TOY
HE'S GUNNA JUMP FOR JOY

CLEAN UP MY HOUSE
KICK OUT THE MOUSE
SETTLE DOWN

GIVE UP THE BOOZE
EAT SOME FOOD
KICK THOSE DRUGS TOO

MAKE THAT CALL
WORK IT OUT ONCE + FOR ALL
AIN'T GUNNA RUNAWAY NO MORE

SEE MY MOTHER
TELL HER I LOVE HER
RING UP MY BROTHER

UNPACK MY BAGS
WASH THESE RAGS
PACK EM ALL BACK
+ GO RIGHT BACK A-ROAMING

DEATH I EXPECT
YOU COMING
DEFEAT
SURVIVE

I'M LYING DOWN LOOKING AT THE SKY
I'M WAITING TO DIE
I'M WAITING TO DIE

~~ABOVE ME~~ I SEE THE FIRST RAYS OF THE SUN ~~SPINNING SUN~~
THE DAYS BEGUN
DEATH HAS GOT TO COME

I HEAR THE MORNING LARK
SINGING IN THE PARK
DEATH WON'T WAIT TILL IT'S DARK

CLOUDS FILL THE SKY ~~[illegible]~~ ~~DARK~~ SUNSET
~~THE SKY IS FULL OF FAT WHITE CLOUDS~~
~~LIKE~~ I'M WAITING TO DIE I'M WAITING TO DIE

I'm gunna buy him a toy
When I get home
He's gunna jump for joy
But right now, right right now
Right now, I am a-roamin'

When I get home
I'm gunna unpack my bags
When I get home
I'm gunna wash these dirty rags
When I get home
I'm gunna pack them up again
And I'm gunna go, I'm gunna go
Right back a-roamin'

Babe, I Got You Bad

Babe, I got you bad
Dreaming blood-wet drams
Only madmen have
Babe, I got you bad
I wish to God I never had
It makes me so damn sad
O babe, I got you bad
Yeah, babe, I got you bad

I long for your kiss
The turn of your mouth
Your body is a long thing
Heading South
And I don't know what I'm talking about
All my words have gone mad
O babe, I got you bad

The seasons have gone wrong
And I lay me down in a bed of snow
Darling, since you been gone
My hands, they don't know where to go
And all my teeth are bared
I got you so much I'm scared
O baby, I got you bad

With a sweep of my hand
I undid all the plans
That exploded the moment I kissed you
On your small hot mouth
And your caramel limbs
Which are hymns to the glory that is you
Look at me darling, it's sad sad sad
Look at me darling, it's sad sad sad
Baby, I got you bad

Smoke billowing from the bridges
And the rivers we swam in are boiling
My hands are reaching for you everywhere
But you're not there, or you're recoiling
A weary moon dangles from a cloud
O honey, I know it's not allowed
To say I got you bad

ST. LUKES ROAD 64

NEWS ITEM

CUMBERLAND NEWS ITEM

TODAY 20th FEB NEWS ITEM

Police track down
and shoot a young LION
in a field of sheep!!!
Where the lion lies down with the lamb

Wine

SHEEP MAY SAFELY GRAZE

Sheep may safely graze
The Wolves have been rounded up + put to bed
Sheep may now safely graze
Have no fear, little one, + rest your worried head
Sheep may safely graze, my boy
Crocodiles have been hunted from your dreams
Sheep may now safely graze
The house has been cured, cuddled and cleaned

Sheep may safely graze
Fruit hangs heavy from the vine

The Bridle Path

Luck kissed my brow and held me close
Said, "I can no longer stay
My brother will watch over you
While I'm gone away"

"You two will get on fine," he said
But he really did not convince
The sun turned grey as he rode away
And I haven't seen him since

"I didn't catch your name," I said
Luck's brother answered so
"My name is Love," he said to me,
"I'm sad to see my brother go"

His teeth were straight and pearly white
His eyes the clearest blue
And when he spoke a second time
His voice was rich and smooth

"Look yonder," said Love and pointed
Then gave a winning little laugh
I saw the prettiest young thing, with a wedding ring
Walk down the bridle path

Opium Tea

Here I sleep the morning through
Until the call to prayer awakes me
And there is nothing to do but rise
And follow the day wherever it takes me
I stand at the window and look at the sea
Then I make me a pot of opium tea

Down at the port I watch the boats come in
Watching boats come in can do something to you
And the kids gather round with outstretched hand
And I toss them a diram or two
And I wonder if my children are thinking of me
For I am what I am and what will be will be
I wonder if my kids are thinking of me
And I smile and I sip my opium tea

At night the sea lashes the rust red ramparts
And the shapes of hooded men move past me
And the mad moaning wind, it laughs and it laughs
At the strange lot that fate has cast me
And the cats on the rampart sing merrily
That I am what I am and what will be will be
The cats on the rampart sing merrily
And I sit and I drink my opium tea

I'm a prisoner here, I can never go home
There is nothing here to win or to lose
There are no choices needing to be made at all
Not even the choice of having to choose
I am a prisoner, yes, but I am also free
'Cause I am what I am and what will be will be
I'm a prisoner here, yes, but I'm also free
And I smile and I sip my opium tea

THE SWEETEST EMBRACE
A Song for Barry
La la la la
A SONG FOR WARREN
2 Songs
P. Maria sv. Škapulíře.
YOUR LOVE CANT HURT ME ANYMORE
a Song for WARREN
"Your Love, your Love, it cant hurt me anymore

The Sweetest Embrace

Our time is done, my love
We've laid it all to waste
One thousand moonlit kisses
Can't sweeten this bitter taste
My desire for you is endless
And I'll love you 'til we fall
I just don't want you no more
And that's the sweetest embrace of all

To think we can find happiness
Hidden in a kiss
Ah, to think we can find happiness
That's the greatest mistake there is
There is nothing left to cling to, babe
There is nothing left to soil
I just don't want you no more
And that's the sweetest embrace of all

O where did it begin
When all we did was lose
There's nothin' left to win

So lay your weapons down
They serve no purpose in your hands
And if you wanna hold me
Then go ahead and hold me
I won't upset your plans
If it's revenge you want
Then take it, babe
Or you can walk right out the door
I just don't want you anymore
And that's the sweetest embrace of all

O where did it begin
When all we did was lose
There's nothin' left to win

It's over, babe
And it really is a shame
We are losers you and me, babe
In a rigged and crooked game
My desire for you is endless
And I love you most of all
I just don't want you no more
And that's the sweetest embrace of all

Index

A

B

C

D

F

G

H

I

J

K

L

M

N

O

Other books from 2.13.61:

HENRY ROLLINS / The First Five
HENRY ROLLINS / See A Grown Man Cry — Now Watch Him Die
HENRY ROLLINS / Get In The Van
HENRY ROLLINS / Black Coffee Blues
HENRY ROLLINS / Eye Scream
HENRY ROLLINS / Do I Come Here Often?
JOE COLE / Planet Joe
DON BAJEMA / Reach
DON BAJEMA / Boy In The Air
BILL SHIELDS / Human Shrapnel
BILL SHIELDS / The Southeast Asian Book Of The Dead
BILL SHIELDS / Lifetaker
BILL SHIELDS / Rosey the Baby Killer & Other Stories
DUSTIN PRESTRIDGE / Knuckle Deep
EXENE CERVENKA / Virtual Unreality
EXENE CERVENKA & KEN JARECKE / Just Another War
IAN SHOALES / Not Wet Yet
IGGY POP / I Need More
TRICIA WARDEN / Brainlift
TRICIA WARDEN / Attack God Inside
MICHAEL GIRA / The Consumer
ROB OVERTON / Letters To Rollins
NICK CAVE / King Ink
NICK CAVE & THE BAD SEEDS / Fish In A Barrel
ALAN VEGA / Cripple Nation
ROSS HALFIN / Fragile: Human Organs
ROSS HALFIN / Metallica: The Photographs of Ross Halfin
STEPHANIE CHERNIKOWSKI / Dream Baby Dream
THE PHOTOGRAPHER'S LED ZEPPELIN
GLEN E. FRIEDMAN / Fuck You Heroes
ROKY ERICKSON / Openers II
JOE CARDUCCI / Rock & the Pop Narcotic
NICK ZEDD / Totem Of The Depraved
HENRY MILLER / Dear Dear Brenda
NATALIE JACOBSON / No Forwarding Address